All day,
fingers to
which she cou
to vibrate from Des's kiss.

Had the morning been as magical as it had seemed? Had she and Des really confided in each other, let each other in on early hurts? Had there been a kind of communion between them, real intimacy, for the first time?

Had he really kissed her as though she were an attractive and desirable woman? Had he promised more, if she wanted it?

And had she really told him she wanted it?

Dear Reader,

Spring cleaning wearing you out? Perk up with a heart-thumping romance from Silhouette Romance. This month, your favorite authors return to the line, and a new one makes her debut!

Take a much-deserved break with bestselling author Judy Christenberry's secret-baby story, *Daddy on the Doorstep* (#1654). Then plunge into Elizabeth August's latest, *The Rancher's Hand-Picked Bride* (#1656), about a celibate heroine forced to find her rugged neighbor a bride!

You won't want to miss the first in Raye Morgan's CATCHING THE CROWN miniseries about three royal siblings raised in America who must return to their kingdom and marry. In *Jack and the Princess* (#1655), Princess Karina falls for her bodyguard, but what will it take for this gruff commoner to win a place in the royal family? And in Diane Pershing's *The Wish* (#1657), the next SOULMATES installment, a pair of magic eyeglasses gives Gerri Conklin the chance to do over the most disastrous week of her life…and find the man of her dreams!

And be sure to keep your eye on these two Romance authors. Roxann Delaney delivers her third fabulous Silhouette Romance novel, *A Whole New Man* (#1658), about a live-for-the-moment hero transformed into a family man, but will it last? And Cheryl Kushner makes her debut with *He's Still the One* (#1659), a fresh, funny, heartwarming tale about a TV show host who returns to her hometown and the man she never stopped loving.

Happy reading!

Mary-Theresa Hussey

Mary-Theresa Hussey
Senior Editor

Please address questions and book requests to:
Silhouette Reader Service
U.S.: 3010 Walden Ave., P.O. Box 1325, Buffalo, NY 14269
Canadian: P.O. Box 609, Fort Erie, Ont. L2A 5X3

The Wish

DIANE PERSHING

SILHOUETTE *Romance*®

Published by Silhouette Books

America's Publisher of Contemporary Romance

To Morgan Rose, an excellent daughter, and George and
Ashley's real mother. Thanks for letting me borrow them.

 SILHOUETTE BOOKS

ISBN 0-373-19657-1

THE WISH

Copyright © 2003 by Diane Pershing

This edition published by arrangement with Harlequin Books S.A.

® and TM are trademarks of Harlequin Books S.A., used under license.
Trademarks indicated with ® are registered in the United States Patent
and Trademark Office, the Canadian Trade Marks Office and in other
countries.

Visit Silhouette at www.eHarlequin.com

Printed in U.S.A.

DIANE PERSHING

cannot remember a time when she didn't have her nose buried in a book. As a child, she would cheat the bedtime curfew by snuggling under the covers with her teddy bear, a flashlight and a forbidden (read "grown-up") novel. Her mother warned her that she would ruin her eyes, but so far, they still work. Diane has had many careers—singer, actress, film critic, disc jockey, TV writer, to name a few. Currently she divides her time between writing romances and doing voice-overs. (You can hear her as "Poison Ivy" on the *Batman* cartoon.) She lives in Los Angeles, and promises she is only slightly affected. Her two children, Morgan Rose and Ben, have completed college. Diane looks forward to writing and acting until she expires, or people stop hiring her, whichever comes first. She loves to hear from readers, so please write to her at P.O. Box 67424, Los Angeles, CA 90067.

Dear Reader,

As planned, I concluded *Cassie's Cowboy* (released in April 2002) with the standard boy-gets-girl-and-kisses-her-a-lot, followed by those magic words *The End*. Which meant the book was done, right? Not quite.

Without any input from my brain, my fingers continued to type away on an epilogue, and I realized that, although I had supplied the reader with the happy ending required in romance fiction, I wasn't quite ready to let go of a key ingredient in that book—the outlandish magic eyeglasses that granted one wish to the wearer. It's not every day you get a shot at making dreams come true, so why not keep the magic alive? And so Cassie handed off the glasses to a tall, skinny, brainy young woman who owned a bookstore.

Her name is Gerri, and *The Wish* is her story. She's a bit of a klutz and socially awkward; she's also funny and good-hearted, and I'd be honored to call her my friend.

Gerri has an unrequited crush on the town's most popular playboy; needless to say, her wish involves making him notice and appreciate her.

However, as the old saying goes, "Be careful what you wish for...."

Enjoy!

Diane Pershing

Chapter One

Sobbing, Gerri ran out of the casino ballroom and into the night as though running for her life, the skirts of her gown flying in the dry evening breeze. Down the flight of stone steps to the street level she fled, but on the second to last step, her heel caught in the hem of her dress, and she tripped.

Cursing herself under her breath for her lifelong clumsiness, and with tears still streaming down her cheeks, she managed to disentangle her heel, avoiding a pratfall—but turning her already sprained ankle— as she landed upright with both feet on the sidewalk. Taking a moment to wince in pain, she took off again at a run, but when she rounded the corner of the building, she ran smack into a very solid, all male chest.

"Oof!" she said.

"Gerri?" the owner of the chest replied, surprise in his voice as he gripped her upper arms to prevent her from taking a header.

"Des?"

Unbelievable. She'd just bumped into Des, of all people, her good friend, or sort of good friend. Incredibly strong and wonderfully solid Des, solid being the operative word here. She'd just barreled into him, all six-feet-in-heels of her, but, bless him, he'd stayed right where he was, upright and planted firmly, so yet one more mishap in an evening of mishaps had been avoided.

Thank God for small favors, Gerri thought. After the social nightmare she'd just experienced, all she needed was another ungraceful, unfeminine, classless, ignominious, *klutzy* act on her part, and she might just as well die on the spot.

The pressure on her upper arms increased. "Hey, Gerri, what's wrong?"

She looked up at him, then glanced away quickly, too uncomfortable to face Des's probing gaze. "Nothing." She shook off his grip and headed out into the night. "Thanks for catching me. I have to go home now."

She was maybe two steps away when he caught up to her and pulled her around to face him. Again, she tried to avoid looking at him head-on, because she didn't want him to see her face, which, as she well knew, was a total disaster. Her inexpertly applied mascara was dripping down her cheeks, her eyes were red, as was her nose, she was sure—she was *not* one of those women who looked beautiful when they cried. She'd long ago bitten off any lipstick she'd been wearing. The week-old bruise on her upper cheek was probably glowing all kinds of colors, making her look like a woman in need of shelter from an abusive husband. Her attempt at a hairdo had come partly loose and was hanging in funny clumps around her face. Her gown was wrong, her shoes were killing her, and although Des had surely never thought of her as anything approaching glamorous, somehow this final humiliation of his seeing her at her very worst was more than she could bear.

"Gerri?" He squeezed her arm, not unkindly, but to get her attention. "Look at me." He followed this with a finger under her chin, forcing her to meet his gaze.

Amazingly enough, he didn't blanch at the sight of her ruined aspect. In the glow of a nearby streetlamp, his craggy face seemed less forbidding than usual, and his startling blue eyes less hooded and mysterious. His eyebrows, black as his thick head of hair, were furrowed, but with concern, not anger. There was no judgment in his gaze, none at all.

A sudden warmth filled her chest area, making her want to cry all over again. Dear Des, the only male friend she'd ever had.

"What are you doing here?" she managed with a lopsided grin, swallowing the urge to weep all over him.

The only answer he gave was one of his noncommittal shrugs. "Tell me what happened," he persisted.

"Nothing," she said brightly, but couldn't keep it up. "Everything." The traitorous tears came barreling up through her tear ducts once again.

He pulled her into his arms, enfolding her, pushing her head against his neck, offering friendship and comfort, both of which she sorely needed at the moment. Still, her immediate reaction was to stiffen. This was the first time the two of them had touched, really, the first time she'd felt the true strength of his long arms, ropy with muscles honed from years of ranch work.

Then she relaxed against him and sobbed into his shirt collar, worrying all the time if her mascara was the waterproof kind that would stain his shirt, but then realizing that the way the stuff had been leaking all over her face answered that question. It was on the tip of her tongue to offer to launder his shirt, but then she told her brain to turn off, please, and just let her rest here, enveloped by the first pair of strong male arms she could remember in years.

However, Gerri's brain was rarely able to turn off—it was her life's blessing and its curse—so she pulled away from him. "Please, Des, don't," she told him, taking a step back and swiping her index fingers under her lower eyelids, trying to soak up the blackness of the makeup. "I don't deserve comfort. I should have known better."

"Known what better? Has someone hurt you?"

Had someone hurt her? How about lots of some-ones? How about the fact that tonight, it felt as though her whole life was one big hurt? "It doesn't matter," she replied. "I'm going home."

Again, she moved away from him and hurried down the street. But again, Des wasn't going to let her go so easily. He walked quickly beside her. "Didn't you go to this charity thing with Rance to-night? Why isn't he seeing you home?"

"Because—" she began, but stopped. It was too difficult to explain.

After all, how could she tell her friend Des that she'd accepted Rance's last-minute, totally unexpected invitation to be his date for a formal charity function because she'd seen it as a golden opportunity? That even though a little voice inside her had told her to say no, she'd said yes, despite her still-bruised face and her sprained ankle, both of which she'd gotten from falling off a ladder in her bookshop?

And how could she tell her friend Des that even with the rainbow-colored abrasion under her eye and a limp, another woman could have pulled it off, could have managed to appear elegant and self-possessed, making a small joke about her less-than-stellar appearance?

But that woman was not Gerri, never had been. She'd done it wrong, all of it. The hour she'd spent at the charity function had been the hour from hell, and had been from the start.

The moment she'd walked into the ballroom, looking, she imagined, like a refugee from the backwoods, her personality—which was often sunny, funny and most definitely friendly—had undergone a total collapse. Even on the arm of Terrance Wallace III, better known as Rance, her self-confidence, which she possessed under certain conditions, plummeted to an all-time low.

She'd wilted under the scrutiny of the town's upper crust. She'd laughed too loudly and at the wrong places, apologized for her behavior, stumbled over her words, even stepped on Rance's foot the one time they'd danced. She'd practically worn a sign on her saying Kick Me.

The coup de grace had been in the ladies' room, to which she'd escaped in an attempt to force her fly-away hair back into its bun. While fussing at the mirror, despair fighting tooth and nail with an inner pep talk, she'd overheard a couple of other guests talking about her from their individual stalls.

The gist of the unflattering and mean-spirited remarks, after they'd done tearing apart her hair, her face, her dress, her body, was that the only qualities she had to recommend her were her sense of humor, her brains, and her ownership of a bookstore. It might be better, they suggested, if she stopped trying to do anything or be anyone else, such as an appropriate date for Rance, the town's most eligible bachelor.

Choking down a sob, she'd run from the bathroom, tripping over her dress as she did, all the voices of a lifetime echoing in her head: Outsider. Different. Brainiac. Plain. Clumsy.

In grade school, she'd been given the nickname of "The Giraffe," because she'd early on developed long, skinny legs with knobby knees and a long, skinny neck—minus the knobs—to match, none of which had changed as she matured. "Giraffe" had morphed into Gerri as she got older, which was a lot better than her given name, Phoebe Minerva, so it had stuck.

But the self-image had stuck, too.

There were other social disadvantages beside physical ones. Her brains put her way ahead of others her age, so she'd skipped a couple of grades and was always younger than her classmates. She didn't develop breasts, for heaven's sake, until she was a senior in high school. Along the way, there had been the occasional date, the rare brave boy willing to take a chance on a girl who was taller and most probably a lot smarter than he was. But socializing with the opposite sex was always excruciatingly uncomfortable, with Gerri trying too hard to relax and the boy trying too hard to impress.

The only one who'd gotten through had been Tommy Mosher, in college. But that too had turned out badly. Very badly. Nearly ten years later, his treachery still hurt, still informed her daily life. Men did not fall for her. Men did not find her attractive. The only thing they might want from her was her brainpower and what it could do for them.

But she still had normal female urges, and even with her history, a kernel of hope remained. Maybe, she'd dreamed over the years since college, maybe one day she would encounter a worthy man who would love her.

She'd had a crush on Rance, a regular customer in her bookshop, for months, so when, earlier that day, he'd asked her to go to a formal event with him, something inside her had screamed, "Here's your chance!" Finally she would erase the past. She would do it right this time. She would feel and act like a princess, gliding easily and gracefully through the evening.

Fool, she called herself now. People didn't change. Sure, the prince had asked her to the ball, but she was no Cinderella, with a fairy godmother who provided magic that would make her blossom and bring her inner beauty to the surface.

Inner beauty? Hah.

"Gerri?"

Des was still waiting for the answer to his question about why Rance wasn't seeing her home. She glanced sideways as they rushed along, his long legs having no trouble keeping up easily with her hurried pace. The expression on his face, which was arresting rather than handsome, with its deep, attractive grooves from spending days on horseback, was stormy. Oh, no, she wondered. Was he angry at her for canceling their date tonight, so she could go to the affair with Rance?

But it hadn't been a real date. Not between her and Des. They were friends, that was all, just a bite to eat together was all it was to be. So why would he be hurt? Still, she couldn't avoid noticing the fact that his expression was fierce and combative now, erasing the genuine concern of moments earlier.

It was confusing. The whole evening was confusing. If only she could do it over.

"Why isn't Rance here with you?" he persisted.

"He doesn't even know I'm gone. You don't have to walk with me, you know," she told him, her voice breaking again. "I just want to go home."

"How will you get there?"

That stopped her in her tracks, while other pedestrians on the neon-lit downtown Reno street hurried past them. She hadn't thought that far ahead. She lived a couple of miles out of town, at the end of a long country road, and didn't have her car with her. "I'll get a taxi."

"I'm taking you."

She could have argued, but didn't have the strength. Besides, she was grateful that the problem was solved. Her stupid heels, and her ankle, were killing her.

In Des's pickup truck, after she'd given him directions to her place, Gerri stared out the window at the black night. As soon as you got outside of Reno proper, you could see all the stars that the casino lights obscured. The vast darkness was soothing, somehow, with its tiny, mysterious pinpricks of light, and had the effect of calming her down.

They drove in silence for a while, the only sound the shifting of gears. Eventually Des spoke. "Should I ask how it went?"

She snorted a quick laugh. "Probably not a good idea."

"It's okay," he said, nodding, "it's none of my business."

"It's not that," she hastily assured him. "But let's just say tonight was not one of my most rewarding life experiences. I'm lucky you showed up."

Why *had* he shown up? she wondered once again. How had he happened to be there, right outside the casino, at the very moment she was coming out? She supposed it had been some kind of coincidence, although she was not a great believer in coincidence.

When she'd asked him about it earlier, he'd shrugged it off. Des was a pretty mysterious man in some ways, and the reason they got along so well was not only that they were both a little off-beat by nature, but also that each sensed in the other areas of privacy which were respected and not pried into.

They'd met because Gerri had been boarding her horse at his ranch for the past half year or so. They'd gotten into the habit of conversing while she saddled

Ruffy and when she came back from her ride. Sometimes Des even came out on the trail with her; they rode together easily, joked and chatted. Correction: She did most of the chatting, he the listening. But there was an ease between them that Gerri—given her dismal history with men—appreciated deeply.

She'd never had a friendship with a man and, although their relationship didn't extend past these morning rides, she didn't want to spoil it. In truth, she'd been surprised that he seemed to enjoy being with her.

After all, Des was a looker, no doubt about it; in town, she'd run into him at the grocery store a few times and she'd seen many a female pause in her tracks when they saw him. She didn't know exactly why he'd chosen her to be friends with, but it was probably because she wasn't after him and therefore wasn't a threat to his single existence. By now, she'd gotten beyond his rugged, decidedly masculine looks and just plain liked the man. If she wanted to know more about him and what made him tick, well, maybe in time he'd trust her enough to open up.

He pulled up in front of her pretty little house, a narrow two-story Victorian, which would have been more appropriate placed on a San Francisco street than up a country road, surrounded by mountains. The moment she'd arrived in town two years earlier, she'd seen this house, fallen in love with its charm and eccentricity, bought it and restored it to its current pristine condition. She'd had a full bank account at the time and still had most of it in careful investments, including the property on which she'd opened The Written Word. Moving to Nevada and owning the bookstore had been a lifelong dream, and now she had both.

Ah well, she thought philosophically, as Des turned off the motor, you can't have it all. Despite tonight's pain and regret and humiliation, it had still been the best two years of her life. She had friends, like Didi and Des, and a business she loved and supported. Her shop had an extensive children's section, so there were always adorable little ones around to talk to and read to. She loved kids; if she never had any of her own, wasn't this a fine substitute?

Before she could put her hand on the door handle, Des was out of the truck and pulling open the passenger door for her. Gerri stepped out, winced for a moment when she landed on her sprained ankle. Again, he held on to her elbow till she regained her balance.

"You sure you're okay?"

"Absolutely. I'm going to soak that stupid ankle in a nice basin of warm water right now." She put a hand on his shoulder, considered kissing him on the cheek, but nodded instead. "Thanks, Des. I appreciate it."

"You're all right to go in alone?"

"I'm not alone. I have George and Ashley."

"Cats aren't a lot of comfort."

"Says the non-cat lover. I'll be fine. And thanks."

As he observed Gerri limping into her house, it was all Des could do not to follow her, scoop her up and carry her inside. She was one stubborn woman, not good at accepting help. Although they were alike that way, he admitted to himself. Independent. Not just independent. Not trusting that if they fell, there would be someone there to pick them up.

Well, he'd been there to pick her up tonight. Good thing, too. Gerri had been through something upsetting, that was apparent. But what? Had Rance said something to her, insulted her? He felt his jaw tighten as he considered it, then he forced himself to relax as she turned at her front door and waved at him before she entered. He waved back, and felt a small flutter in his chest region as she winced once more before closing the door behind her. That ankle of hers was killing her and he knew it.

He got back into his truck and slammed the door shut. Why did this particular woman get to him? He never let anyone get to him. He'd kept himself detached from others and their needs for a long time. But lately, Gerri had gotten under his skin, and that made him uneasy. He wished he could turn it off. It was dangerous to get involved with others. He'd learned that lesson a long time ago.

"Damn," he muttered, then backed the truck up, put it in gear and headed out to the highway toward his spread. In a way he was glad she'd canceled their dinner plans tonight, because he'd been on the verge of saying something to her, something he was sure he'd regret. It wasn't easy, feeling so…vulnerable to any woman. Who knew what he might have said, what he might have regretted the minute it popped out of his mouth?

His reaction when she'd canceled on him, however, had not been one of relief, not in the least. In a breathy voice, she'd called and said Rance had invited her to this fund-raising event and she hoped Des wouldn't mind, as they'd had casual plans, at best. Was it okay? she'd asked him, sounding apologetic and excited at the same time.

Sure, he'd told her, no problem. She didn't have to know about the jealous rage that filled him when he hung up. Rance? That vain, spoiled excuse for a human being? Des was being replaced tonight by him?

The strength of his reaction took him by surprise. Scared the piss out of him. He hadn't felt that kind of emotion since Stella had run out on him. Amazing. All these years later, and he still hadn't managed to exorcise that possessiveness, that *passion,* from his makeup.

It was that same passion which had led him to head downtown, a couple of hours earlier, to stand on the street outside the casino where the fund-raiser was being held, not sure why he was there or what he would do or say if he ran into Gerri and Rance. Time and again, he'd told himself to go home, but he couldn't seem to make himself leave. Bewildered by his lack of control, he'd paced. And waited.

And been rewarded, at least, by being there for Gerri when she needed him.

Disgusted with himself, Des shook his head then hit the highway, eager to get back to his ranch. He was better there, with his animals and his books, and his little secret of what he did to unwind, the secret that no one else on earth knew about.

Tonight he'd been about to let Gerri in on his secret, which was foolish. He'd been about to trust her. What a laugh. So, yeah, it was good that she'd canceled on him. More than good. It was a kick in the pants, a warning. It was better this way, best to cut it off before it had a chance to breathe.

So then why did he feel like taking his fist and punching his dashboard? And why wouldn't the picture of Gerri's mascara-smeared, bruised and grief-filled face leave his head?

Gerri kicked off her shoes and plopped down on the couch, sighing with relief. Who was the monster who invented high heels, anyway? She was too tall as it was. Didi was always telling her that she should be proud of her height and not slump over as though she'd committed a sin just by existing.

Didi. Wait till she heard about tonight's debacle. Tomorrow, though. There'd be plenty of time tomorrow for girl-type analysis and dissection.

A small *meow,* followed by a deeper, bolder one, let her know the babies were aware she was home. Their paws padded over the hardwood floors; in the next moment, both George and Ashley were on her lap. Or one of them was. The other was on her thighs. And both were purring.

It was dark in here, she suddenly realized. She reached over to turn on the lamp when her hand brushed against an object on the side table. The light revealed the object as her bizarre pair of reading glasses.

She picked them up and stared at them, then had to smile. They were the ugliest pair of spectacles she'd ever seen—milky turquoise, fan-edged with rhinestones all over. Like something a female impersonator might wear when assuming the character of a

gossip columnist or the president of the garden-
ing club.

Still, they were special because the children's author Cassie Nevins had given them to her at the first
book signing Gerri had held in her newly opened
shop, nearly two years ago. At the time, Cassie had
confided that the glasses were magic: if you rubbed
them and made a wish, you'd more than likely get it.

Gerri's belief in magic rated right up there with her
belief in ghosts and time travel, which was not at all,
so she'd discounted Cassie's claim. But tonight she
smiled at the plastic frames, turned them over in her
hand and stroked both cats with the other. Ashley, the
huge gray-and-white longhair had, as usual, gotten
pride of place on Gerri's lap. George, smaller, sleeker
and black as night, managed to find purchase on her
narrow thighs, his front claws digging just a little bit
into her dress. Fine with her, Gerri thought. Dig away.
She'd give them the damn thing to play with to their
heart's content.

"What do you think, guys, huh? Should I wish for
something?"

Well, duh. The obvious thing would be to wish that
everything this evening had gone differently, that her
fantasy of being Grace Kelly in her twenties, reincar-
nated, would be granted. But she'd still have to deal
with the bruised face and the limp.

"Okay," she said out loud, rubbing her thumb over
the earpiece and smiling at her silliness. "Why not
make a wish, right? What can I lose?"

She took another moment to gather her thoughts.
All the awfulness had started a week ago, when she'd
fallen off the ladder, so...

She took in a deep breath, then said, "Here's what I'd like. I wish I could go back to the moment before I fell and do the whole week over, knowing what I know now."

She added for emphasis, "And this time, I'll do it right."

Chapter Two

She got her wish. Just like that.

There was no drama about it, no breath-robbing, head-spinning whirling through space, no dramatic drumrolls, no eerie voices or otherworldly music. It just…happened.

One minute Gerri was sitting on her couch at home, petting her cats, and the next, *poof!* she was perched on the ladder in her bookshop, in the exact position she'd been in last Friday evening, looking for an arcane book on ancient Aztec tattooing rituals for an elderly customer currently waiting on the phone. Rance stood at the foot of the ladder, as he had then, talking to her about his family, complaining some, making some jokes, generally chatting with her as he liked to do now and again, using Gerri as an available ear.

"Mother is really getting into this whole I-want-to-be-a-grandmother thing. You know, we-need-heirs-for-the-family-name, and you-aren't-doing-your-part. On and on. Like she did about six months ago. Back then, if you recall, I managed to distract her by taking that racing car course, which about drove her crazy."

"That would certainly do it," Gerri found herself replying, just as she had that night.

Inside, however, her mind was doing its own speed laps. She had to hold on tightly to the sides of the ladder to keep her balance. As her eyes couldn't seem to focus, she wasn't able to read the words on the books' spines yet. Dear God, she thought, her heart rate accelerating, her mind filled with confusion, wonder, even some terror.

What was going on here? one part of her asked, even as the other part answered promptly. *You just made a wish by rubbing a pair of ugly reading glasses. You are now where you were a week ago. Ergo: The wish has been granted.*

Even so, her scholar's mind shifted through alternate possibilities: she was in the middle of a dream, one of the wish fulfillment types that Freud had written about in his seminal work, *The Interpretation of Dreams,* in which the dreamer incorporates her daily worries or fantasies into a story, one that allows the dreamer to continue sleeping, achieving needed rest. Or...

She was hallucinating. Gerri pinched her upper arm, and it hurt. She gazed down and Rance was still there. So, no hallucinations. Or...

Someone was playing a joke on her, had snuck up behind her as she sat on the couch at home, conked her over the head, hauled her here, placed her on the ladder, arranged for Rance to be in attendance.

Not likely.

But then…how…? Was she really *here,* back through the time-space continuum, to exactly one week ago?

There was one sure way to check it out. She ran her fingertips over her cheekbone. No pain, no swelling. The shop's round security mirror hung just to her left, so she leaned in to peruse her image. Nope, no discoloration or bruises. Just her extremely average face, with its hazel eyes, pale eyelashes and brows, a sprinkling of freckles across an average nose, a mouth of no particular distinction, except it wasn't too large or too small.

But no swelling or redness in the least. The evidence of her accident had been with her all week, but right now, there was none. And her sprained ankle? To make sure, she put her weight on her right foot as she balanced on the ladder rung. No pain, no weakness there.

So, then it was the week before. Had to be.

Her mind reeled, searching and discarding one more time, all kinds of other theories: sci-fi ones like an alternate universe or a time machine, mathematical ones like relativity gone berserk, malformed logarithms. Logical explanations like…

None. There were none, no other explanation. Except the one that she knew, in her gut, was *the* one.

The magic glasses worked. Her wish had been granted. Period, end of discussion.

It was like someone had pressed the rewind button on a videotape, to the beginning, instead of fast forwarding to the end, which in her case had been the dreadful dinner dance and her making a total fool of herself.

She would get to do the week over.

She closed her eyes. Thank you, thank you, *thank you!* There was to be a reprieve from Gerri the klutz, the social misfit, the tall, brainy woman unfit to be on the arm of Terrance Wallace III. Now, cautiously, she even allowed a small ray of hope to shine inside. Maybe, if she was *very* careful, and paid a lot of attention to her behavior this week, maybe, just maybe, the prince would finally notice the existence of the right princess for him, even though she'd been part of his universe for what seemed like years and he hadn't gotten the message yet.

Only one year, of course, since Rance had come into her shop, searching for a coffee-table book for his uncle's birthday, but in that year, Gerri's fantasies and dreams had been filled with him.

The subject of her thoughts was complaining again. "I don't know what kind of distraction I can give Mother this time. I don't intend to marry yet, if ever. And any grandchildren are way in the future. I'm only thirty-two, for Pete's sake."

"Maybe you should tell her that."

"That I'm thirty-two?"

She grinned down at him. "That marriage is way in your future. You're pretty independent, so let her know."

"Done it and done it. Doesn't get through. Hey," Rance said with a speculative gleam in his eye, "you and I would have great kids, know that? With my looks, which I'm told are passable, and your brains, which are off the scale, the kid would be a major winner. Mother would finally shut up.''

On that previous Friday night, the one before ''the wish,'' Rance's remark—even tossed off as lightly and mockingly as it had been—threw her. She'd been flattered that he'd even thought of her as a woman. In fact, her always-overactive brain had conjured up a picture of the physical act involved in making children. With Rance.

That graphic image had made her lose her balance. She'd slipped off the ladder, bruised her cheek on one of the rungs and had badly sprained her ankle. For the entire next week, she'd had to wear an Ace bandage and soak her foot morning and night. She'd missed riding her horse Ruffy, missed her nice morning visits with Des, hadn't seen or heard from him all that week, in fact, until he'd called up on Friday afternoon and casually suggested they grab a sandwich together that evening.

And last week, needless to say, she'd looked *awful* at the ball.

Not this time, Gerri told herself. This time she would get to do it right.

''You know,'' she found herself replying to Rance with a lightness that matched his, ''a famous actress once said something like that to George Bernard Shaw. She suggested they have children together because with her looks and his brains, their offspring would rule the world. 'But, madam,' he replied, 'what if they had my looks and your brains?'''

When that got a nice chuckle from Rance, Gerri congratulated herself on reacting with sophisticated badinage instead of taking a header off the ladder.

Her fingers skimmed along the spines of the books
on the top shelf—where she kept the most old, rare
and valuable books—until she came upon the object
of her search. "Aha!" she said aloud. "*Native American Origins of the Art of Tatau,* by Reginald
D'Olivier, Ph.D."

"Sounds weird."

"Not to those who care about skin painting," she
said, and pulled it out.

"You're just full of comebacks tonight, aren't
you?" Rance said, finally getting off his favorite subject of himself and grinning up at her in appreciation.

Again, she met his gaze, noted those sea-green
eyes, that slightly shaggy dark blond hair that fell
rakishly over one eyebrow, that *GQ* model's perfectly
chiseled face. And for a brief moment, she was unable
to speak.

Then she shook herself, made herself say lightly,
"I feel amusing tonight."

"But that book looks heavy enough to hold down
a tent. Want some help?"

No, I'll manage.

The words were almost past her lips, but she
stopped them before they made the journey to the
outside world. Of course she could do it herself, she
could do everything by herself. But wasn't this a
chance to appear just a bit, well, feminine? Not help-
less, not in the least, but at least willing to let the big
strong man help with what men did so well—lifting
things?

This was another test, another chance to do it differently, to practice being…what?

A flirt and a liar?

No, to allow someone—a male someone—to help her. To not be so darned capable of taking care of herself that men rarely offered to let her lean on them.

She closed her eyes for a moment, saying a silent prayer of thanks to whatever power had arranged for this wish. She would try to be worthy, she promised. *She would do it right this time.*

"Thanks," she told Rance. "If you'll take the book, I can manage me."

Gerri stepped down a rung, carefully this time, placed the book into Rance's outstretched hands and watched him set it down on the counter. Then turning around again, so she could keep her balance, she began to descend even more slowly and was surprised to feel two hands around her waist, helping her to the floor. As he lifted her, she waited for a telltale grunt. She might be slender, but her height made her weigh more than a typical woman.

But he wasn't even breathing hard as he set her down on the ground. She was afraid to turn around to thank him, afraid that his touch had set her cheeks to flaming. Due to her treacherously pale skin, she had never been able to hide it when she was embarrassed.

"Merci," she managed, keeping her back to him.

"Hey, my momma raised me to be a gentleman," he said into her ear, then turned her around to face him.

Now her nose was two inches from his, their mouths close enough to kiss. She knew her cheeks were bright red, but she managed a dry response. "And to give her grandchildren, it seems."

"Ouch. Don't remind me," he said with a grin that

was both charming and self-mocking at the same time. How was it, she wondered, that some people managed to make the smallest movement attractive, made it look so easy, when others had to struggle all the time just to appear part of the human race?

She'd been pondering that same question since early childhood and had come up with no solid answer yet. But at least now she was safely on the ground.

Did it! Gerri congratulated herself silently. Got down that ladder and no accidents, no bruises. She might even have appeared graceful. Well, probably not. Or perhaps, to be kind, as graceful as she could be, which was not very. And Rance hadn't seemed fazed by her weight, gave no outward sign of having developed a hernia or back spasms. Yay for our side.

She picked up the book, hurried behind the counter, and picked up the receiver. "Dr. Albright? I've got it." She listened to the retired professor's pleased response then said, "Yes, the third edition... Well, thanks, I'm so glad I could be of help." She felt a huge grin split her face as the elderly man went on about how long it had taken him to locate the tome, and what a treasure Gerri's shop was, and how grateful he was that the young woman had decided to settle here in town, filling a void in the community.

Last week, there had been nothing like this response. Gerri hadn't found the book by the time she'd slipped off the ladder, and poor Dr. Albright had been left on hold for quite a while, while she tended to her wounds.

"Yes, I'll hold it for you till tomorrow. Just ask for it at the cash register."

Rance watched her, an expression of amused affection—the way you looked at a pet—on his face. When she hung up, he said, "You're terrific, you know that?"

She wrinkled her nose, felt her face coloring again. "No I'm not."

"No, really, you're such a, I don't know, a *giving* person. It makes you so happy to help others, your face glows with it."

"Enough," she said, waving his compliments away, and loving them at the same time.

He walked to her side of the counter, reached behind her, and yanked at her ponytail. "If I had a sister, I'd want her to be just like you. Well, I have to head out. See you," he said and headed for the door.

As her inner mind was repeating the sister remark, most definitely at the top of the all time kiss-of-death-to-a-future-relationship remarks, she asked, "Where to?" careful not to let her disappointment show.

"Gotta go meet a plane."

"Oh?" She already knew the answer to her next question. "Who's coming in?"

"Marla Connelly," he said with a cat-who-got-the-cream grin.

"The model?"

"Yup. I met her in New York last week. She's looking to buy some property for a ranch. I've offered to show her around town a bit." He raised his eyebrows in a Groucho Marx way, indicating his plans would go a bit further than just showing the lovely, sophisticated woman around town.

A wrench of jealousy hit her gut, just as it had last week. But...wasn't everything supposed to be different? Hadn't she been granted the chance to do it right this time?

Wait, she reminded herself. The ball— No, she amended quickly, not "the ball." She really needed to stop using fairy-tale vocabulary. The charity dinner dance a week from now, that was what she was supposed to do right. It was there that Rance would finally see what had been under his nose all along. Lovely, sophisticated Princess Gerri.

"Well, go on then," she said, accompanying him to the door. "See you soon."

Through the glass she watched him walk away until he was out of sight. Pleased with herself at having at least avoided injury, Gerri turned around and nearly fell across a carton of books that were still waiting to be shelved. Whoops, she said silently as she righted herself against the counter. Lesson number one—you can go back in time, but if you're a klutz, you're a klutz, magic or no magic. Good luck with that one, she thought sardonically, as she carefully steered her way around the carton. It would take more than a miracle to make her graceful.

SATURDAY: The morning was magic. Ruffy was in fine, frisky shape today as they cantered toward the hills where the sun was just making an appearance, casting all kinds of lovely colors over the distant Sierra Nevadas and the plains below. Gerri was full of hope this morning, having slept well—no pain from bruises that weren't there, no ankle twinges, no aspirin or ice necessary. Last week she hadn't been able to ride, but today she could. She was wondering if Des would be joining her, as he often did in the morn-

ing, when the sound of horse's hooves behind her told
her that the man himself was making an appearance.
She slowed Ruffy down to a slow trot and waited for
him to catch up with her.

"Hi," she said as he joined her.

He nodded his greeting. A man of few words, was
her friend Des. The laconic, solitary rancher who
never said more than what was absolutely necessary.
She liked that about him, especially as he never
seemed to mind her chatter.

He trotted easily beside her. "Beautiful day, isn't
it?" she said, inhaling a deep lungful of cool morning
air.

"Uh-huh."

"Race you to the tree!" She took off before he
answered, knowing that her mount didn't have a
chance against his sleek black gelding, but going for
it nevertheless. Within moments, he'd caught up to
her and passed her, but kept just ahead of her instead
of racing off into the distance, as he most certainly
was capable of doing.

They ran the horses for fifteen minutes or so, until
Des pulled up at a grove of cottonwood trees, the
tallest of which leaned over the edge of a babbling
creek. She'd come to think of it as their tree and had
since the day months before when she'd dismounted
here to adjust her stirrups and he'd ridden by, stopped
and asked if he could help. She'd accepted gratefully
because, back then, this whole horse thing had been
new to her.

Born and raised in New York City into a family of
academics and intellectuals, Gerri's only previous experience with equines had been to watch mounted po-

lice during parades and to observe the aging, over-
worked animals that pulled carriages around Central
Park. But she'd always been fascinated by the
beasts—their sturdy musculature, the grace of their
necks—and had vowed to have her own one day. And
to learn to be a good rider.

After eighteen months in the Reno area, Gerri had
bought Ruffy and boarded her at Des's place, which
had been recommended to her by the horse's previous
owner. She'd taken a few lessons and was now, if she
said so herself, not bad, and getting better.

Thanks to Des. In his quiet way, he'd helped her
learn how to saddle her own horse, how to watch out
for tree roots and the occasional snake as she rode,
how to water and brush her mount at the end of the
ride. He hadn't had to do all that, she knew it, and
thought he must be a very kind person to have taken
the awkward city slicker under his wing.

"Whoa!" she said now, pulling up next to him.
She was as out of breath as Ruffy must be, but happy.
"That was fabulous!"

"You're doing fine," he said, "getting better and
better," he added, just the hint of smile on his usually
stoic face. Beneath his well-worn cowboy hat, she
observed, not for the first time, his startling blue eyes
and the lines radiating out from them, formed by
years in the sun. Black hair and blue eyes. Black Irish
coloring, he'd told her once, in a rare moment of talking about himself. His people had come to America
during the potato famine and had led a hardscrabble
life. He'd bought his ranch about five years earlier. It
was small, but he worked hard, and she had a sense

that he, too, was fulfilling a lifelong dream of having a place—even an identity—of his own.

She was naturally curious about his personal life. He wasn't married, she knew, and lived alone. But there was an air of privacy about him that didn't invite personal questions, so she hung back from prying. Once in a while, like when he stared at the mountain range to the east, she got a sense of loneliness, even a shadow of sadness, in the man. But mostly he seemed comfortable in his solitary existence. Except he seemed to enjoy her company when they rode together, which was once or twice a week in the mornings.

For the first time in her adult life, Gerri felt *comfortable* with a man. Consequently, when she was with him, her behavior was relaxed, not forced. He had the gift of making her feel good about herself, accepted her for what and who she was. All her life, Gerri had tended to say whatever was on her mind; as she had a really *busy* mind, poor Des had received an earful of opinions on books, ideas she'd read about and been mulling over, politics, new scientific breakthroughs, an interesting new word, the little miracles of daily life. She spoke to him sometimes of her past unhappiness, of not fitting in, of being too tall, too clumsy.

She'd never gone so far as to tell him about Tommy, her one unhappy love affair, but it still amazed her how she felt free to share just about everything else with him. Occasionally, she would stop and ask if she was talking too much, and always he said not at all, that he enjoyed listening to her. Once he'd even called her "a breath of fresh air."

Bless him, she thought now, bless Des for opening a new world to her, one where men and women could be friends. She'd always had female friendships, but his was the first with the opposite sex, and she valued this relationship.

"One of these days," she said with a grin, "you're not going to be able to beat me so easily."

Again, that small hint of smile. "I believe you."

Together they sat on their horses while the animals grazed a bit on the nearby grass, Gerri gazing at the creek's rushing waters and the way the rising sun glinted on it. Her heart felt so full this morning—the wish had made all kinds of new things possible. Suddenly she wanted to tell Des about that wish. She had to share the miracle with someone, for heaven's sake. It was too good to keep to herself.

"Des, do you believe in magic?"

He squinted his eyes. "Magic?"

"Yes. You know, the kind where you say an incantation and all of a sudden you get this thing you've always wanted? Or you go to bed one way and wake up the next morning, different?"

He gazed at her for a few moments, considering her question. Then he shrugged. "I believe in what I can see and touch, Gerri."

"So, you're not into, you know, a parallel universe or communing with dead souls or the power of the unknown?"

"Afraid not," he said, one side of his mouth curving upward slightly. "Why?"

No, she thought, not Des, the ultimate pragmatist. Maybe Didi, her friend who owned the antique shop next door to hers. Didi might be the one to tell about the miracle. "Just wondering. I'm always wondering about something, I guess."

"I like that about you," he said simply. "Ready to head back?"

Des, too, was wondering, but it was about what was going on in that furiously busy brain of Gerri's. She seemed different this morning, exhilarated, somehow. Not that she wasn't always pretty upbeat, but there was something about her, some…inner light.

A thought struck him then that made him scowl. Rance, he bet. He knew about her crush on him, even though she'd never actually said anything about it. When she talked about the good-for-nothing playboy, even casually, she usually blushed and got a stupid grin on her face. She thought she was in love with him. Des had never heard her say it, but some women, despite having good brains and common sense in most areas, fell for that kind of pretty boy who flirted and never stayed put, who promised and never followed through.

His ex-wife had been like that. After three years of marriage to Des, Stella had been lured away by some fast-talking agent type who'd seen her singing backup in Harrah's lounge and told her he'd make her a star. Last Des had heard, she was waiting tables in L.A., and waiting for her big break.

It had probably not been a good match in the first place: a man who loved ranching and a woman with a decent voice and stars in her eyes. Still, Des didn't have a lot of faith in the staying power of the female sex.

Gerri was different, though. He wasn't quite sure how to categorize her, only knew that, over the

months, she'd become more important to him than
he'd intended. Whenever he realized it, the emotion
not only took him by surprise, but scared the pants
off him.

He was better off alone, that much he knew about
himself. He was not what was known as a good com-
municator. Sometimes he tried to stay away when he
knew she'd come to ride, but mostly he couldn't seem
to stop himself from riding out to meet her. He enjoyed her company. Hell, she even made him laugh
sometimes, which was rarer than rare for him. Just a
few minutes with Gerri and some inner tightness always eased up.

Unless, of course, she mentioned Rance. Then he
found himself tightening up all over again.

"I'm dying of thirst," Gerri said suddenly. "Let's
get back so I can gulp down some water from your
barn hose."

"No need," he found himself saying, "come to the
house. You can have a glass of water there."

He saw the look of pleased surprise she gave him,
and wondered himself how that one had popped out.
He'd never invited her to his place, had never invited
any woman to his place, not since Stella had taken
off. It was his sanctuary, his cave, and being invaded
by another human being—most of all a woman—was
tantamount to losing a piece of his soul. Still, he'd
said the words and it was done.

"Well, sure, thanks," she said with a grin. "I'd
love to see where you live."

"Don't expect much," he warned.

"If you're afraid I'll be one of those fastidious
'house beautiful' types, forget it. I'm pretty messy

myself, and my knowledge of home decor stops at what color to paint the walls, white or beige.''

He chuckled. How could he not? She was so self-effacing, so open about what she considered her multiple shortcomings. Over the months he'd heard about them all. He wondered if she'd ever had a boyfriend, wondered even if she was a virgin. A twenty-nine-year-old virgin? In this day and age? He'd never asked. If he had, it would have opened the door to her asking all kinds of questions of him.

Gerri had seen the outside of Des's place before. It was a one-story, white stucco building with a tiled roof and large windows. Now, as he opened the door and she walked in, she was totally captivated by what lay within. The living room was cool after the heat from the morning sun, and was furnished with a cozy-looking couch and matching armchair, adjacent to a large stone fireplace. The floors were of natural-colored hardwood, dotted by several small Native American print rugs. Two of the walls were lined with floor-to-ceiling book-filled shelves. This pleased her inordinately. She had no idea Des was a reader; he'd shared none of that with her.

Off to the right was an archway leading to a hall-way that seemed to be the bedroom wing. To the left was another archway, and it was through this he showed her to a warm, yellow-tiled kitchen. A scarred round wooden table with two chairs sat in the middle of the room under a ceiling fan.

"This is great," Gerri enthused. "It's so homey, Des," she went on, "so comfortable."

When he shrugged, she figured her compliments embarrassed him a bit. He went to the sink, got a glass from a long shelf over it, and poured her some water. She took the glass from him eagerly and downed it quickly. "More." She handed it back to him. "I feel like I've been drained of all bodily fluids this morning. Might be the anchovies I had on the pizza last night."

One eyebrow went up as he refilled her glass. "Anchovies, huh? You're one of the only women I've ever met who likes them."

"You, too?"

He nodded. "Anchovies, pepperoni and mushrooms."

"Yes!" she said, pumping her fist in the air. "The big three. We need to get a pizza together sometime!"

Something in his gaze withdrew as she said this, and she knew she'd overstepped a line somehow. "Sorry. Did I say something wrong?"

"No, of course not," he said. Then frowning, he added, "Why do you do that to yourself?"

"Do what?"

"Apologize. Assume you're in the wrong."

"Do I? Darn, I thought I'd gotten over that."

He reached out a hand and she had the feeling he was going to stroke her cheek, but the moment passed and he dropped his hand to his side. "Sorry. It's not my place to criticize you."

"Of course it is. Now, who's apologizing? We're friends, aren't we?"

Again, that shadow of something hidden behind his eyes. "Yeah, we're friends. It's just that you're a terrific woman and you shouldn't put yourself down."

Terrific woman. His words warmed her. He really was the most special man. And it was true, she'd always put herself down, apologized for making anyone feel uncomfortable all her life. She'd tried, really tried, since coming west and starting her new life, to cut that out. But old habits, and old scars, ran deep. It would probably take a lobotomy to change her.

"Well," she said, "thanks for that. I wish I believed it," she added ruefully.

Inwardly Des cursed himself for snapping at her. Why had he said that? Because he cared about her, dammit. She *was* terrific, and he wished she knew it, could take it in.

An awkward silence descended over the room, so Des gestured toward the table. "Um, you want to sit down? Rest for a few minutes?"

"No," she said brightly, "but I'd love to look at your books. May I?"

Then she was off to the living room, walking slowly along the shelves, oohing and ahing in that enthusiastic way she had. "Look!" she said. "You have all of Dickens. And Thomas Aquinas. And, oh, Des, so many volumes of poetry! Frost and Wordsworth, and look here, Rilke's *Duino Elegies.*" Hands on hips, she turned to him. "Why didn't you tell me?"

"Tell you what?"

"That you're one of us. The word-lovers. Especially the poetry. How come I never knew that about you?"

Her enthusiasm made him feel even more awkward; he was already nervous about her being there. He wanted her to like the place, while at the same time he was kicking himself for caring. The woman knew too much about him already.

"It didn't come up," he said with a shrug.

"Sure it did. How many mornings have I bent your ear about new authors, especially poets, I'd been reading? And you just sat there on your big horse and nodded politely. Des, you're a fraud."

She said it with a grin, so he didn't feel attacked. And she was right. She didn't know, couldn't know, how much of a secret life he'd led always, disguising his love of reading from his family because they would have laughed at him, called him names. He'd kept his books under his bed, read them with a flashlight way into the night, while everyone else slept.

"I don't have much education," he told her.

"Formal, you mean. Obviously you've educated yourself which, in my opinion, is a whole lot more meaningful. You read because you want to, not because you have to, like you do in school." She snapped her fingers as an idea came to her. "You have to come to the shop on Tuesday night. We have poetry readings, you'll love it. Why haven't you ever come to my shop, by the way?"

He'd been there once, Des could have told her, and had seen her mooning over Rance, which had irritated him, so he hadn't been back.

"Say you'll come," she persisted.

"I usually do paperwork in the evenings."

"Try. Okay?"

He couldn't help noticing the eagerness, the openness of her expression. Once again, he shrugged. "I'll see."

Chapter Three

SUNDAY: Gerri figured there was probably some kind of shopping gene she'd failed to inherit, because, quite simply, she hated the act, especially when it came to trying to pick out clothing for herself. She tended to dress simply, in blouses, skirts and loafers or jumpers and loafers. She knew she had little taste and no real sense of style; her skills were verbal and mathematical, and most definitely, *not* artistic. And apart from her lack of taste, it always seemed a waste of time because she never found just the right thing to make her look or feel more attractive than she knew she was.

"It's an inside job," her mother used to tell her. "Beauty is from within." But Gerri always knew her brilliant and beautiful mom said that to make up for the fact that her daughter had gotten the worst of the family traits, physically, anyway: her mother's intelligence, pale skin and freckles, but not her thick red hair, normal height or buxom, womanly body. Her father's brain, plus his height, straight brown hair and a tendency to resemble a stork, but not his piercing gray eyes or regal nose. The co-mingling of DNA had worked out fine for Gerri's brother Ned, who was handsome and tall and, of course, brilliant.

Still, Gerri knew she'd been lucky in her parents. In their large apartment on Central Park West, there had always been a lot of love and enthusiastic encouragement to pursue any interest she developed. The nightly dinner table discussions were lively and expressions of affection were constant. She'd traveled extensively and been given a lot of personal freedom. She knew her values were pretty solid, knew that when you wanted something, really made up your mind to have it, you needed to work very hard. There wasn't a lazy bone in Gerri's body and, self-perceptions aside, she had a real can-do attitude.

It was armed with this same attitude that she attacked the mall at opening time. She'd probably need all day to accomplish her mission. What a blessing that Didi had agreed to meet her here! This morning on the phone, Gerri had told her friend that she needed help choosing a dress and Didi had agreed, pleased that Gerri was showing some interest in fashion at last.

Of course, Gerri hadn't yet been invited to the fund-raiser this coming Friday, but if that happened— and if the wish parameters continued to be followed, it would—by heavens, she would be prepared this time.

What she'd worn that night just before "the wish" was—she winced at the thought—the bridesmaid's gown she'd been forced to buy for her brother's wedding three years earlier. Even at the time Gerri had known it wasn't the right color or cut for her, but Corrine, Ned's intended, had wanted pale pink chiffon with lots of ruffles, and what the bride wanted, the bride got. Gerri knew in the dress, she looked like someone had covered a telephone pole with crepe paper bird plumage.

Needless to say, if she'd had time to get something else last Friday night, she would have. But Rance's invitation had given her an hour to get ready, so her options had been limited.

This time, she was determined to find the *perfect* dress and have it hanging in her closet, ready to go. She'd buy some cosmetics, maybe even have her makeup done so she could learn, for once, how to make the best of whatever assets she did have. Was it time to go to a hairdresser and get her hair cut and styled, even dyed?

She always wore her fine brown hair back in a ponytail because it had no body. In high school, she'd tried regular rollers, hot rollers, a curling iron. But always, the defiant straightness won out within minutes, no matter how much effort she expended. Once she'd had a perm and what a disaster that had been! No soft, springy curls for her. No, every tendril had stuck straight out from her scalp, made a dismal effort at a wave, then stuck out some more toward the sky. She'd worn a cap for months until the perm grew out.

What miserable teenage years hers had been, she thought with a rueful smile of remembrance as she perused the shop windows, trying to see herself in that cute little running outfit or the long, form-hugging, slate-gray evening gown. Probably not. The dress required hips and breasts to look like anything other than a sack. And she wasn't possessed of much of either.

She was prevented from plunging into gloom by a cheerful voice behind her shouting "Hold up there, *amiga!*" and turned to see Didi waving at her, speed-walking as she approached.

A small fireball of energy, Didi Garcia always hurried, in everything she did. Barely five feet tall, she had the broad, sturdy build of her mixed Native American and Hispanic ancestry. She was habitually twenty pounds more than the recommended weight, although her extra poundage didn't seem to keep men away. Didi was never without a boyfriend if she wanted one, but so far, no one had gotten her thinking long-term.

She and Gerri were the classic "opposites-attract" kind of friends, in that one was tall and skinny, one short and broad. One had a lot of college, the other had none. One was city-bred, one small town. One was uncomfortable with men, the other wasn't. But they also had a lot in common, including the ability to make each other laugh and curiosity about people and what made the world tick. Also, Didi had business goals, the way Gerri had. Her shop, Ramona's Closet, sold both American antiques and Native American art, and was quite successful. Like Gerri, she put in ten to twelve hours a day at her business. Her parents had toiled as field hands and fruit pickers, their work seasonal and nomadic. Early on, Didi had vowed never to work for anyone but herself.

They'd become immediate friends the first day Gerri moved into the bookshop, and Didi came over from next door asking what she could do to help. Now, two years later, it was like Gerri had known her her entire life. There was nothing she couldn't tell Didi, and now she couldn't wait to let her in on "the wish," and to ask for her help making it come true.

"So, what's all the hurry about finding a dress?" Didi asked as she fell into step beside Gerri.

Instead of answering her, Gerri stopped in front of a display window and pointed to a long, pale green dress hanging on a sulky-looking mannequin. "How would I look in that?"

"Like you were on the verge of tossing your dinner. Come on, tell me."

"Why can't I wear that green?" Gerri complained. "It's so pretty."

"Because your *gringa* skin tone won't react well to it. Trust me on this one. Now, what do you need a dress for?"

Gerri tore her gaze away from the sophisticated gown, then looked around to make sure they weren't being heard. Grabbing Didi's arm, she said, "Let me buy you a cup of coffee and I'll tell you."

When they were seated, each with a doughnut and coffee before them, Gerri got right to it. "Do you believe in magic?" she asked, as she had Des the day before.

"What kind of magic?"

"You know, the fairy-tale kind. Where you make a wish and it comes true?"

Didi took a sip of coffee, then stared at her over the rim of the cup. "Haven't given it much thought."

It was a start, Gerri thought; at least her friend hadn't laughed at her. She tore a piece of doughnut off and rubbed it between her thumb and forefinger. "Your ancestors believed in magic, didn't they?"

"Not fairy tales, no." Didi took a bite of her doughnut and chewed it thoughtfully. "But, yeah, they had spells and incantations for the harvest, stuff like that."

"And do you, I mean, as a modern representative of your ancestors, do you still believe in that?"

"What, are you interviewing me?" Didi cocked her head to one side and studied her friend. "What are you getting at?"

"Well, you're going to think me crazy—"

"Hey," she interrupted with a laugh, "I already think that, so get to the point."

Gerri swallowed the lump of apprehension that had suddenly lodged in her throat. It would sound insane, it had to. But, this was Didi, her dearest friend, and if she couldn't trust her dearest friend...

"On Friday night, I'm going to a formal fund-raiser. With Rance."

Didi's eyes opened wide with shock. "You're what?"

"You heard me. I'll be his date, and I have to get a gown and makeup and deal with my hair and all that. That's why I asked you to meet me here."

"Let me get this straight. Rance asked you out?"

"Well," she began, rolling the piece of doughnut into a tight little ball, "not exactly. But he will."

"Oh, Gerri...."

At the sight of the compassion filling Didi's eyes,

Gerri felt her old defensiveness come right to the fore. "I know. I'm not good enough for him."

"Wrong. You're *too* good for him."

"No, really," she protested. "You don't know him. He's really an okay guy."

"Underneath that egotistical rich-boy facade, you mean."

Gerri sighed. "Okay, you don't like him, I get it."

"Hey, I don't care about him enough to like him or dislike him. It's his type I don't like." Didi gestured impatiently with one hand, dismissing Rance. "But what's this about Friday night? Has he asked you or hasn't he? And what's with all the questions about magic?"

When Gerri didn't answer right away, Didi offered her a sardonic grin. "Okay, confess. You made a wish on a star that he would ask you out, right?"

"Um, well, not exactly. But you're close."

Now her friend's face registered confusion. A long silence passed between them before Didi expelled a large sigh, pushed her doughnut to one side, and said, "Okay, let's hear it. All of it."

"Promise you won't laugh."

"Promise."

Gerri began eagerly. "Remember when Cassie Nevins came to the store to sign books?"

"The children's author? Sure. Nice lady."

"Yes. She gave me a pair of reading glasses."

"Those turquoise things that look like something from a 'How to Be Ugly' catalog."

"Right. Well, Cassie told me the glasses were magic."

"Magic," Didi repeated. "Okay, I'll bite. What do they do that's so magic?"

"You make a wish. And it comes true."

"Uh-huh," she said with overt skepticism. "And so you took those glasses and you, what? Made a wish that Rance would invite you out, to some kind of formal thing?"

"Exactly. Except that he already did. Ask me, I mean. And I already went. Sort of."

"Excuse me?"

"It was last week, the thing, the fund-raiser. Or this coming Friday. It's the same, really."

"The same." Now Didi studied her like she was a new species that might or might not fly off somewhere.

It was Gerri's turn to expel a sigh. "Look, I know I'm not making a lot of sense, but it's all true. The thing is," she barreled on, "last week I slipped and turned my ankle and had bruises on my face and wore this hideous dress and went to the fund-raiser and it was a disaster. And so I asked the glasses to let me do the week over and they granted me that, so I'm redoing last week. See? No bruises, no tape on my ankle." She paused, out of breath.

"When did you get hurt? I don't remember that."

"Last week."

"You didn't tell me about it, and I think I would have noticed something like that."

"That's because it hasn't happened yet, last week I mean. Or it did, but not really. Oh, dear."

Gerri knew from Didi's reaction that she wasn't making sense. And, really, how could she blame her friend, because how could you find the words to explain the situation so it seemed logical? They were dealing, after all, with a total absence of logic, which meant the usual dialectical reasoning didn't work.

All she could do was shrug helplessly. "I don't know how to tell this so you'll believe me."

There was a softening in Didi's dark brown eyes. "Gerri? *Amiga?* Are you okay?"

"Yes."

Her friend reached across the table and set her palm on Gerri's forehead. "No fever. I don't know, have you been taking drugs? Not the illegal kind, I know you're not into that. But maybe you mixed medications or something and you're having a reaction."

"No. I'm telling you the truth."

The sight of her friend's distress on her behalf made her try one more time to explain. "Didi, have I ever done this before? Have I ever come to you with a story like this, ever?"

"No."

"So you know I'm not usually hallucinatory or anything like that, right?"

"Yeah, but, well, let's face it. Your IQ is pretty high, and they do say that the line between genius and madness is pretty thin. Not that I'm trying to insult you or anything, but maybe something has tipped the scales, maybe you went over the edge and don't know it."

Rather than take her theory as an insult, Gerri wondered if the idea might not have merit; certainly it wasn't a possibility she had considered.

Was she mad? Had she crossed over into the land of illusory psychosis? But even as she asked herself the question, she knew the answer. No. She had real, tangible memories of her fall from the ladder, the bruised face in her bathroom mirror. And she'd known conversations before they occurred—known Rance was going to wonder about the children they would have, and that he was meeting Marla Connelly at the airport, both prior to him telling her.

No, she wasn't mad.

But it had to appear so to any rational human being. If she were in Didi's chair, she'd have the same fears for her friend as the ones her friend was now having for her. Clearly the theory of magic glasses strained credulity to the breaking point.

There was too much concern now, even a hint of fear, in Didi's usually cheerful countenance. She had to make it go away, so she offered up a smile. "Look, just forget I even mentioned it okay?"

A moment went by before Didi said doubtfully, "Were you pulling my leg?"

"Just forget it, okay?"

"But—"

"Please," she urged. "Pretend the conversation never happened. And do me a favor, help me find a dress, give me some advice on makeup. I want to be prepared when…if I ever do get asked out to something formal. Humor me."

"You do know that formalwear costs a lot."

"There's still a little left in the bank account, and besides, it's time I spent some of my money on new clothes. Aren't you always telling me that? Come on."

Des sipped his Scotch and stared at the leaping flames in his fireplace. He was feeling out of sorts, fidgety, and had hoped the drink would calm him down some. It had been a bitch of a day. He'd had to put down a horse who'd broken a leg, and had yelled at his foreman for small things that weren't the man's fault at all. He'd ridden Major till the gelding was near to exhaustion, then he'd stomped on foot over his acreage, finding fences that needed mending, loco weed that hadn't been pulled. It wasn't like him to be this agitated, but he'd be lying to himself if he said he didn't know the reason for it.

Gerri. Tall, skinny, brainy, foolish Gerri Conklin. He couldn't get her out of his head, couldn't stop thinking about the fact that, as she'd stood in his kitchen yesterday morning sipping water, it had struck him that she looked good there, even that she belonged there, with him, bringing all the laughter and gaiety and downright enthusiasm for life that the woman possessed, and which he knew he was sorely lacking.

"Damn," he said aloud to the fireplace and took another sip of his drink. She wasn't even his type. He liked women who know the score and expected nothing of him. Since Stella's departure there had been a few easy, short-term relationships that ended just as easily, with no one hurt, no one asking for commitments. Gerri wasn't like that; she was too damned fragile when it came to men. Nothing with her would ever be easy, or short-term.

But when had it happened, this growing attraction he felt for her?

He'd been amused by her that first day he'd come upon her talking to her horse, sharing her confusion about how the stirrup worked with the animal, as though it could let her in on the mysteries of saddles. Amused and touched, actually, by the sight. So out of her element, yet good-natured at the same time.

Later on, riding along with her, coaching her some, she'd seemed so…sweet, was the only word he could come up with. On subsequent rides, he'd been in awe of Gerri's brain and the way it hopped around in its quest for answers. He'd always been somewhat embarrassed by his lack of education, especially when he was around really smart people, but not with her. He liked her brain, was fascinated by it.

She, in turn, seemed to respect his commonsensical attitude toward the complex questions she was always mulling over. Once, she'd told him she was aware that she tended to make situations more complicated than they needed to be. Over the weeks of their relationship, there had grown a mutual respect for each other's gifts, and he was now totally comfortable during their talks.

How did she feel about him? That was the million-dollar question. But he already knew the answer. They were *friends*. He winced at the word. Often she told him how *comfortable* she felt with him, how being with him made her feel *at ease*.

This was not the vocabulary of someone interested in him romantically, or even just plain sexually. Besides—he growled as he took another slug of his Scotch—her feelings were involved elsewhere. Rance. Des muttered a curse. Rance Wallace, the third in a line of Rance Wallaces. He knew the man only casually as their paths rarely crossed, but there was little doubt that he was a good-for-nothing who had always had it too easy, both in life and with women.

Poor Gerri. There was no way Rance could return her crush. No way he would look at her and imagine her in his life. The man was a fool not to see the uncut gem who pined for him, but if there was one thing Rance had to have in his lady friends, it was beauty. Not to mention a good fashion sense and breasts; he went for well-endowed glamour girls, always had. Gerri didn't even come close.

Des's hand tightened on his glass till he realized that he might break the damn thing, so he set it down.

It was a lost cause. Not only because Gerri didn't think of Des as a potential love object, but because he knew, in his gut, that he was wrong for her. He had little heart left to give. He didn't trust women, didn't trust them to stay the course, through good times and bad. He knew he was defective that way, but his childhood and, later, marriage to the one woman he'd allowed past his defenses, had made him into what he was. People didn't change their basic makeup; that much he knew through a lot of hard knocks and life experience.

Then why couldn't he get Gerri out of his head? And where was all this possessiveness when he thought about her coming from?

And what was he going to do about it?

Gerri sat slumped on her couch, stroking George and Ashley, nursing her sore feet. Shopping was exhausting, and she and Didi had shopped. And shopped.

And *shopped.*

Gerri had tried on what felt like hundreds of dresses, all kinds of colors, all styles. Her friend had insisted she check out one with a short, tight skirt, saying if she had legs like Gerri's she would definitely show them off. But in the mirror, all Gerri could see were knobby knees and large feet. After Didi sighed in exasperation, they went on to longer styles. In the end they wound up with a black, long-sleeved, ankle-length, silk dress.

The shoes were another problem. Her narrow feet were hard to fit, but finally she purchased a pair of silver sandals with one-inch heels. Didi had tried to talk her into three-inch stilettos, but Gerri didn't want to appear even taller than she was.

Didi had protested. "Be proud of your height," she'd pleaded. "Or make a wish on those glasses of yours and give me four of your inches. You can keep the rest."

Gerri had remained firm.

Finally Didi had promised that if she actually went somewhere in the outfit, she would come over and do her hair and makeup for her. That had reduced Gerri to tears of gratitude. "Really?" she'd said. "You'd do that?"

"Well, of course I would," Didi had responded forcefully, her hands on her hips. "Listen, the way you've been carrying on, you've even got me believing this thing on Friday will happen."

"It will, I promise," Gerri said, sniffling.

Didi threw up her hands in exasperation. "You are just a bit *loca, mi amiga,* but then maybe I think the world can use more crazy people."

Tonight, as George purred loudly, urging her fingers to the spot behind his ear that he so loved her to scratch, Gerri couldn't help smiling at her friend's parting words: "Take care of yourself, okay? I mean, if you start hearing voices or anything, call me. I'm always there for you."

Gerri closed her eyes, grateful for friends, grateful for her new life. Now, she could indulge in a favorite fantasy: She and Rance entering the ballroom, his hand under her elbow as they glided confidently into the room, both of them so sophisticated, so elegant.

But for some reason, the picture wouldn't conform to her fantasy. Tonight, it wasn't Rance's face she saw next to her. It was some other man's.

It was…Des.

Des?

But Des was a friend.

The phone rang, interrupting her reverie. She picked up the receiver on the table next to the couch. "Hello?"

"Gerri? This is Des."

Chapter Four

He waited for her response, a curious thumping in his chest area as he did.

"Des?"

She sounded surprised to hear him. And who could blame her? Their friendship so far had taken place entirely on horseback. This was the first time he'd called her. Swallowing the last of his scotch, he answered, "Yes. I, uh, wanted to know what time that thing is on Tuesday night."

"That thing?" She still seemed somewhat distracted. "Oh, you mean the poetry reading?"

"I'm sorry, did I get you in the middle of anything?"

"What? Oh, no. I was just…well, drifting off, you know, in my head."

"How unusual," he said wryly, and was rewarded by that nice, full-throated laugh of hers.

"Familiar territory, for sure," she acknowledged

ruefully. Then, like that, she was back to her old enthusiastic self. "But tell me, will you be there Tuesday night? That would be terrific."

"Maybe. I'm not sure. I just wanted to know what time it starts."

"Seven-thirty. We serve tea and cookies."

"Gee, just what I've been missing all my life. Tea and cookies."

She laughed again. "Now, Des, they're very good cookies."

He, too, chuckled. "I'm sure they are. I was just teasing you."

"Of course you were. I'm so glad you'll be there."

"I didn't say I would—"

"Right, right," she assured him, "you're just finding out, in case, right? But, oh Des, it's such a wonderful evening. It's all about words, lots of them, a veritable cascade of words. Amazing, *interesting* words. It always makes me wish I could write poetry."

"'Cascade of words' isn't bad."

"Borrowed. From one of our regulars. No, I'm there to appreciate. The world needs appreciaters just as much as it needs creators. So say you'll come."

"You're relentless."

"Yup, relentless. That's me."

A sudden silence came out of nowhere, interrupting the easy flow of dialogue. His gaze flickered to the dying flames, then to the mantel, then back to the fire, as he tried to think of what to say next. "So, who usually shows up at this thing?" was all he could come up with.

She answered eagerly. "All kinds of people. You

never know. Amateur poets and some of my regular customers. We even get tourists, believe it or not. The hotels have been nice enough to include our little Tuesdays in their 'Around Town' brochures. Once in a while we get a visiting real, live, professional poet, and we listen worshipfully at his or her feet.''

''What about Rance? Does he ever show up?''

It was out of his mouth before he even knew he was thinking about it. Damn, he muttered silently, as all kinds of recriminations flooded his consciousness.

Busted. Exposed. Naked, for all the world to see. What could have possessed him to ask that? She had to know now. Hell, there was no way he could have disguised his distaste for the man, or his jealousy about her feelings for him.

''Rance?''

Her tone seemed to indicate that she hadn't taken his query as anything more than a casual one.

''Nope. Well, not so far,'' she added. ''I don't think he's interested in poetry particularly—although I'm working on him. Why do you ask?''

Why had he asked? God, she was such an innocent. Did she have any idea that Des's interest in her was more than platonic? And, more to the point, did he even want her to know that it was?

''Nothing,'' he muttered. ''Forget I said anything.''

''Oh.'' After a moment, she sighed. ''I guess you don't care for Rance, either.''

''No, no, really, forget it, okay?''

But she was continuing her thought. ''I know that a lot of people have trouble with him because of his reputation. I mean, I guess he's a bit of a play-boy—''

And shallow and untrustworthy and a lot of other things Des could have said, but kept his mouth shut.

"—and my friend Didi has the same opinion. But I see something in him, well, something that wants to come out but can't."

This was weird, Gerri thought, discussing Rance with Des. After all, there she'd been, fantasizing about one of them—Rance—or rather trying to fantasize about him, when the other's—Des's—face had intruded. At precisely that moment, Des had called. And now the two of them were talking about Rance.

Rance and Des. Des and Rance. Definitely weird. In fact, the timing was awfully coincidental. Too coincidental to be a coincidence, if that made any sense.

But Des couldn't have known she'd been thinking about Rance. So, what was going on here? Was there some more-than-the-eye-can-see explanation she ought to be seeking?

Her mental exploration was interrupted when Des said, "Look, I have to go now. Got an early-morning appointment with a guy about a used truck."

"Oh. All right. Good night, then." She almost added *Sweet dreams,* but stopped herself.

But Des hadn't hung up yet. "Will you be out to ride tomorrow?"

"Sure will," she said cheerfully. "Will I see you there?"

There was a fraction of a pause before he answered, "I'm not sure. Good night." He hung up abruptly, as though eager to get off the phone.

Afterward, Gerri sat for a while, continuing to ponder the conversation, both the unexpectedness of it and her pleasure in it. She went from there to the nature of coincidence, the theory of life-as-timing, and onto "the wish," the subconscious meaning of fantasies and her new black dress and silver shoes, until her mind called time-out for overinput and she climbed into her high, four-poster bed, George on one side of her and Ashley on the other.

She loved the warmth generated by the cats' soft, furred bodies, and tried to remember if a man's body generated the same warmth. It had been such a long time—nearly ten years—since she'd experienced lying next to a man, that she'd nearly forgotten.

Tommy had sure scarred her, hadn't he? But the ending of that affair had only been the final nail in the coffin for her; romantic entanglements weren't for her, ever, she'd decided back then. So she'd shut down, afraid of being used again, hurt again. And now here she was, once again interested in someone who wasn't right for her.

The truth was that, wish or no wish, Rance and she were deeply, profoundly unsuited to each other. She sighed heavily. Deeply unsuited. If and when her wish was granted, if and when they ever got together, if ever he saw past her exterior, and wanted to explore a relationship with her, they would make each other miserable. They had totally different backgrounds, values, interests, totally opposite mental and physical attributes....

She sighed again, causing Ashley to uncurl herself with a tiny *mew* of protest and resettle herself in the opposite direction. It had seemed so important, so...life and death, on Friday night, to make this "Cinderella at the ball" thing happen. Now she had the dress and the shoes and the promise of glamorizing help from Didi, and somehow, tonight, it didn't seem quite as important, as earth-shaking, as life and death as it had seemed just two evenings ago.

And it was downright uncanny how Des had called tonight. Weird, she thought again, as she drifted off to sleep. Weird, weirder, weirdest.

MONDAY: She was headed back to the barn on Ruffy when Des finally made an appearance on Major, galloping toward her from the direction of the river. As he drew closer, his horse's hooves pounding dust into the air, she experienced an unexpected moment of panic. But that was quickly replaced by a lovely warm sensation flooding her bloodstream. God, she was glad to see him.

Gerri usually called out a jovial "Hi!" when she greeted Des in the mornings, but now a strange sort of shyness, a self-consciousness that reminded her of dances at high school, overtook her.

"Good morning," he said almost formally, tipping his hat and slowing his mount to keep pace with hers.

"Yes, it is a pretty day, isn't it?"

He gazed off at the distant mountain range, his Stetson slanted over his eyes. "I think we're due for a little rain."

"Yes, you can smell it in the air."

"Uh-huh."

"We sure do need rain," Gerri said brightly. Good heavens, they were talking about the weather like strangers meeting in an elevator. "I've never ridden in the rain."

"I'd avoid it, if possible."

What was next? she wondered, the stock market? The UNLV basketball team?

"Thanks," was her brilliant comeback.

Flicking the edge of his Stetson with his forefinger, Des said, "Gotta go, Gerri. It was nice seeing you." And he took off, away from the corral she was headed for, and down a dirt road that led to several outbuildings. She watched his retreating back, puzzled and vaguely hurt.

Out of nowhere, it seemed, the chemistry between them had changed. He had been awkward with her, had practically run away from her at the end. There had been none of their usual ease with each other, the friendly banter of the past couple of months. It was as though a wall had dropped between them suddenly, and neither of them had known how to scale it.

It must have been the phone call last night that had changed their dynamic. Had she said something to upset him or hurt him? She played it back in her head. Had she pushed him too hard about coming to the poetry evening?

Maybe Des had just lost interest in her as a friend.

Or—she thought ruefully—maybe she wasn't the most important thing in his life at that moment. There might even be an emergency that needed taking care of, one that caused him to act distracted and in a rush. Yes, that was a much better solution than any of the previous ones, so she'd go with that one.

Still, whatever his attitude toward her had been, Gerri had been a conversational zombie with him. And she knew why.

Not only had he called last night at the precise moment she'd been thinking about him, but this morning she'd awakened at the tail end of a dream about him.

She blushed as it came back to her, in full Technicolor. Before she'd opened her eyes, she'd been dreaming of Des as he sat on his horse. Her mind's eye had perused him, head to toe. It had noted the interesting shadows cast on his rugged face by his Stetson, especially the hollows beneath the cheekbones. The way his broad shoulders took up all the room available in his denim shirt, and how the open neck revealed black-as-night chest hair, not too thick, not too sparse, just right.

That easy slouch of his as he sat in his saddle, the way his long fingers held the reins loosely and gracefully. The way his muscular thighs clasped his horse's withers and how his faded jeans fit so tight she could discern the mound between his long legs.

As the dream faded into reality, and as she'd opened her eyes, Gerri had found herself...aroused. Her skin felt hot and there was an ache between her legs that was both painful and pleasurable.

Turned on by a mental picture of Des on a horse.

How Freudian could you get?

Now, a couple of hours later, she had to wonder how she could be feeling this way about two men at the same time? She was, by nature, monogamous, even if it had been years between crushes.

But...wait a minute. *Was* this also her reaction to Rance? The question had to be asked, because for nearly a year now, Rance had been the focus of her fantasies. Did he—to get right to the point—did Rance turn her on?

As she dismounted and led Ruffy to his stall, Gerri realized she didn't know the answer to that one. Odd. She dreamed of him favoring her with that sly, winning smile of his, of entering a room on his arm and heads turning. She'd thought about winning his love.

But did he turn her on? Did she *want* him, the way a woman wants a man?

Or…did she want him to want her? Period?

Not an attractive picture, if it was so. She didn't care for what that indicated about her self-esteem. Did she really need someone else's high opinion of her in order to feel worthy of love?

All these questions were most unsettling. Usually Gerri didn't shy away from self-analysis, but right now, she decided to shelve this subject. It made her uneasy.

Besides, she had a shop to open, books to unpack and a day to get on with.

TUESDAY: There was a light turnout, eight people only, for tonight's poetry gathering, probably due to the rain. Ten minutes ago, Gerri had stopped sneaking glances at the door to see if there would be a ninth. Richard Mullins, eighty-nine years of age and cantankerous, had just finished, to polite applause, one of his odes to canaries. Gerri was ready to serve tea and cookies when she heard the sound of the door opening and the *ding dong* that announced a customer.

When she turned to see Des standing in the doorway, she experienced the most insane leaping of her heart. He'd spruced himself up and he sure looked good. He wore clean jeans and running shoes, a well-worn, rain-spotted leather jacket over a crew-neck blue sweater. She'd never seen him in civilian clothes, she realized.

Which was why the sight of him without his Stetson threw her. His thick dark hair looked like it had recently been cut, his tanned face was clean-shaven and, basically, he looked gorgeous. The only thing wrong with the picture was that his expression was grim. The man looked as though he were about to enter a dentist's office for a three-pronged root canal with no Novocaine.

Telling herself not to overwhelm him by gushing, she hurried over to him with a smile. "Hi, Des. I'm so glad you could come."

He looked down at his feet momentarily, then back up at her, never cracking a return smile. "Yeah, well, I'm a little late."

"Actually I think we're just about done hearing all the poetry for the evening. But you're in time for those cookies I told you about."

"Oh." The furrow between his clear blue eyes deepened. "You mean, the reading part of the evening is over?"

She shrugged. "No one else has anything to read."

"I do." It came out defiantly, almost angrily.

The force of his declaration made her take a step backward as her hand flew to her throat. "Excuse me?"

"I would like to read something." Then, a little

less fiercely, he added, "Something I wrote." In the next moment, indecision replaced aggression. "It's nothing much. I mean, it can wait," he finished up lamely.

Good heavens, Des had written a poem and was a mass of nerves about reading it!

"No, it can't." Taking his hand, Gerri pulled him over to the makeshift stage, a platform in the center of the room that contained a music stand and a side table on which were water glasses and a pitcher.

Unaware of their conversation, the others in the room were gathered at the counter, where a large plate of cookies resided. "Anything else you need?" Gerri asked him. "Would you prefer to sit? I'll get you a chair if you'd like."

There was a slight tremor in the hand he raked through his hair. "I'll stand, I guess."

Idiot! Des silently called himself. Jerk! Why was he subjecting himself to this humiliation? Why didn't he just turn right back around and go home, the way a voice inside of him was screaming at him to do?

Because, dammit, it was time to pull off the mask. Time to go public, to stop hiding behind grunts and three-word sentences. He'd been writing poetry for twenty years, and no one, not one living person, had ever seen any of it. He would be thirty-five years old on Friday, and if a man couldn't grow up enough to be unguarded, to be *known,* just a little, then when could a man do it? On his deathbed? Like his dad, who'd told him he loved him for the first time five minutes before he died?

His hands fisted and unfisted a couple of times before he was able to gather up the courage to speak again. "I'm not sure I can do this, Gerri," he admitted sourly. "I'm afraid my voice will croak."

"First time?"

The look she gave him was warmly understanding and, bless her, not in the least bit condescending. When he nodded, she smiled. "You're supposed to be nervous the first time. And, believe me, everyone here has been through it. You're among friends."

Friends. Yeah, right. He scowled again, but, still smiling, Gerri added, "I'm honored that you've chosen my shop for your first time." The sincerity shining from her pretty hazel eyes made him able to breathe, at least. She squeezed his hand quickly, then turned to the people milling around the cookies, clapping her hands for quiet.

"Hey, everyone, we have one more poet tonight—" She glanced over her shoulder. "It is a poem, isn't it, Des?"

"I don't know what it is," he mumbled.

There was a small ripple of laughter from the others, and he relaxed just a bit more.

"Well, everyone, this is Des—" Again, she turned around to ask him, "Is it short for Desmond?" When he nodded, she went on, "This is Desmond Quinlan and this is his first time reading, so let's listen."

Hopping off the platform, she moved toward a chair just a few feet in front of him and sat down. The others wandered over and found seats, too, until Des was faced with a small sea of upturned, expectant faces.

Better get it over with, he told himself, before he

changed his mind. He pulled the sheet of paper out of his back pocket, unfolded it, swallowed, licked his dry mouth and began.

In the evening
when the un-world colors shift and change like shadow puppets snared in a wind storm
In the night
when black becomes a living, aching thing and darkness swallows hope
In the morning
when bright white light casts healing warmth on the night's foul dregs
In the daylight
when sharp angles slice through the unforgiving, merciless glare
In the evening
Again
when all the hours have mounted onto each other, one by one by one
and the shadows come
Again
I think of her
And I despair

For a moment, no one said or did anything. Then, as though someone had punched a button, applause erupted. Enthusiastic applause, continuing even as his small audience rushed up to him, one at a time, with compliments. The nervous sweat on his face dried up, and an amazing adrenaline rush of exuberance came over him.

He'd done it! He felt like Rocky on the top of the stone steps, fists in the air with victory.

As he was being clapped on the back, he glanced

over in Gerri's direction. She remained in her chair. The initial look on her face was one of shock. Then a broad smile replaced the shock and she, too, jumped to her feet and came over to him.

A woman with dyed red hair and a booming voice introduced herself as Wilma Fontana. She shook his hand enthusiastically. "That was quite good," she told him as though bestowing a judgment directly from The Mount. "I'm curious. Did you have a real woman in mind when you wrote that? Or was it, perhaps, directed to a symbol, to Everywoman?"

Des stifled a laugh. His heart still raced with this strange excitement. "I'm not talking," he told her, which got appreciative chuckles from the whole group.

No one needed to know it was about all the women in his life, in general, and Gerri, in particular. No one needed to know he'd been working on it, off and on, for a couple of years and that, last night, when he was bursting with feelings he didn't know how to handle, he'd finished it.

Finally it was Gerri's turn. She threw her arms around him enthusiastically and gave him a quick hug. Then, as she was drawing away, he wrapped his arms around her and pulled her back into that hug.

At first she seemed to stiffen, but then she let it happen and relaxed against him.

She felt good, very good. Skinny, sure, but solid, too. She smelled good, too, like lemon-scented body lotion. No perfume, just lemons. He liked the feel of her small breasts against his chest, liked the way her height made her head fit onto his shoulder without either of them having to stoop over or reach up. Closing his eyes, he spread his hands over her narrow back, urging her even closer. A nice fit all around, he thought. A really nice fit.

Gerri's mind was blank—a first, probably. But her skin was reacting in strange and wonderful ways to this body-to-body contact with Des. She could sense his excitement, and felt a bit overwhelmed by it. And by him.

None of this had happened last week, none of it. Shaken, she withdrew from his embrace. The hug hadn't been personal, she told herself, but had come from all those emotions roused by reading his first poem in public. Still, she couldn't keep herself from evading his gaze as she said, "That was excellent, Des, really excellent…your poem, I mean." She reddened some, but forced herself to look him in the eye. "I am amazed, astonished, and altogether blown away."

There was a twinkle in his eye as he bowed slightly in acknowledgment. "I'm pretty sure that's an exaggeration, but thank you, ma'am. It means a lot."

She was about to grab his hand, but thought better of it. "Come," she said, leading him away from the others and toward the front counter, "have some refreshments. I wish I had something stronger than chamomile tea," she went on as she heaped a small china plate with cookies and handed it to him.

"Hey, it's okay." He watched her pouring liquid from a real English tea set. "I'm kind of high from just getting up there and reading."

"So I noticed." She took his cup and saucer over to a small table next to an armchair and set it down. "Well, you're really, really good, and why haven't you ever told me about this? Sit,'' she told him, indicating the chair, then perching herself on the arm.

His legs did feel a bit shaky, he had to admit, so he lowered himself onto the overstuffed cushion, set the plate of cookies next to the tea, and leaned back, willing the tremors in his body to go away. The chair felt great. As did being in the proximity of Gerri's left thigh and buttocks, balanced right next to his forearm.

Again, he was aware of that nice lemon smell of hers. ''I kind of write this stuff for myself,'' he said, answering her question.

''Have you been doing it long?''

''Yeah, I guess so.''

What would she say, he wondered, if he just grabbed her and pulled her onto his lap?

To hell with wondering.

''Des!'' Gerri cried as he yanked her off the chair's arm and on top of him. ''What are you doing?'' She fought to get up again, but was no match for Des's hands on her waist, urging her backward.

''Stay right where you are,'' he told her with a grin. ''You feel good.''

''But—''

''Shh,'' he said. ''Just sit still.''

He noted that the tension remained in her body, so he brought his hands to her shoulders and kneaded them. ''Oh, that's wonderful,'' Gerri said, slumping into the curve created by his lap.

''Good.'' Continuing to massage her neck and shoulders, he whispered in her ear. ''This is my reward,'' he told her, ''for being brave.''

''But I'm too heavy,'' she murmured.

"Not in the least."

"Are you sure?"

"Relax."

But his massage had already accomplished that, so he wrapped his arms around her again. She wiggled a little to settle herself. Uh-oh, he thought. Dangerous move, there. The male organ had a mind of its own, and even if he hadn't meant the act of pulling her onto his lap to be overtly sexual, try telling that to his hormones.

She seemed completely oblivious to the increasing hardness between his legs. Should he be relieved or insulted? he wondered with a smile.

Gerri, never quiet for too long, was talking again. "Have you written a lot of poems?"

Removing one arm from around her waist, he reached over for a cookie. "I guess…about a hundred or so."

"A hundred!" She sat up suddenly and angled around to face him. When he groaned, her hand flew to her mouth. "Oh, God. Des! Did I hurt you?"

"No, no," he lied, wishing he could reach down and adjust himself, but there was no graceful way to do it, especially at a poetry reading where tea was the cocktail of choice.

But Gerri had already jumped up, probably uneasy with physical intimacy. Was it possible she really *was* a virgin?

Or maybe it was intimacy with him.

Like that, his upbeat mood evaporated. Rance, he thought. She wouldn't have reacted that way with Rance.

Gerri's mind was no longer blank. Now it was reeling. So much had happened in the last ten minutes, and all of it a total surprise. Des had come to the reading and had read a poem which had moved her deeply—not only the imagery evoked by the words, but the pain behind it. It was clear he could put on paper what he was unable to verbalize in life.

One surprise followed another when he'd hugged her and then pulled her onto his lap. Not only had they never been physical with each other before, but he seemed so much lighter and more playful than she'd ever seen him.

Now, he was scowling again. Why? What had happened?

She hunkered down so they were eye to eye and rested a hand on the chair's arm. "I didn't hurt you?" she asked him, concerned.

"No, not at all."

"Then why do you look like you're in pain?"

He paused, then chuckled. "It was nothing, promise."

"Well, good, because I have a proposition for you."

He sat up straighter now, one eyebrow raised, his frown totally gone as his blue eyes lit with amused interest. "Proposition?"

More blushing. Really, why couldn't she have had an olive complexion? "No, no, not that kind of proposition."

He snapped his fingers. "Damn."

"Des, really, listen to me." She stood again, unable to stay in one position and not sure what to do with her hands. Being in Des's presence tonight was making her restless. He seemed so different, so not Des, she wasn't sure how to act.

"You may not know this," she said, "but I have a small poetry press. I'd love to see some more of what you've written. Maybe we could talk about my publishing your stuff."

"Wait a minute, aren't you getting carried away?"

"Maybe. But I doubt it."

"You'd want to read all of them?"

"Yes. Will you at least entertain the suggestion?"

The furrow between his brows deepened again, while he thought about it for a while. Then his expression cleared and he favored her with that half smile of his. "How about if we have dinner and talk about it?"

"Dinner? With you?"

"No, with an elephant. Yes, with me." He rose abruptly to face her, making her take a step back. "A business dinner, if you prefer it that way."

"If I prefer it—?"

He studied her, then shook his head slowly. "You know what?" he said softly, a hint of frustration in his blue eyes. "For a woman with a brain that travels at warp-speed, you can sure be slow sometimes."

More confused than insulted, Gerri could only stare back at him. She had no idea what was going on. This was all uncharted territory.

Last week, before "the wish," none of this had happened. There had been no shopping trip with Didi, no morning rides with Des because of her sprained ankle. No phone calls from him, except for that casual, last minute "let's have a sandwich" invitation on Friday afternoon.

Last week the poetry night had ended with Rich and his canaries. There had been no Des coming through the door, revealing this whole other side of himself, this real, live, gifted poet.

Last week she hadn't dreamed about him.

His invitation to dinner had been the latest surprise. But, in truth, it pleased her. But he'd made it about business, and that disappointed her.

If she thought Des was showing quicksilver mood swings, she could match him, swing for swing.

"Gerri?"

For some reason, she found herself fixated on his mouth. He had such nice lips, not thick, not thin, just kind of…generous. Sensual, even. Why hadn't she ever noticed his mouth before? How, she couldn't help wondering, would it be to kiss him?

"Gerri?"

Des was waving a hand in front of her face now. Embarrassed about being caught head-tripping—as the hippies used to call it—she forced herself to snap out of it. "Sorry. What were you saying?"

"I was saying that I'd like to make it on Friday."

"Make what on Friday?"

"Dinner. It's my birthday."

"Your birthday! Well, of course I'll g—" She stopped herself in the middle of the word.

Friday. Oh, no. Not Friday.

Rance was going to ask her out on Friday, for that night.

Or was he?

Nothing else about this week had gone the same— would that be true on Friday, too?

"I'd love to spend your birthday with you," she

said. She touched his arm briefly then snatched her hand away and rubbed it down the side of her jumper. ''I mean, thank you for asking me. It's just that—'' She paused, grimaced.

''Do you have other plans?'' There was tension around those nice lips of his, and she felt like squirming.

''I'm…well, I'm not sure.''

''When will you be sure?''

She noted how the muscles of his jawline kept clenching and unclenching, which meant she must be making him angry. In turn, she felt guilty, although she wasn't sure she deserved either emotion.

''Des,'' she said, nodding. ''I will spend your birthday with you. Yes. I will.''

Instead of looking pleased, his eyes narrowed with suspicion. ''You're sure?''

''Yes. Of course. Yes,'' she said again, making herself sound as firm and reassuring as she could.

But some of her inner struggle must have showed because he shrugged and said easily, ''Hey, birthday or no, it's just two friends discussing business, remember? No need to get all uptight about it. Just friends, okay?''

Chapter Five

WEDNESDAY: Gerri took Ruffy out the next morning, and kept looking around for Des, but he never showed up. Maybe that was for the best. She'd been mulling over all of last evening's events and was now hopelessly confused. What had Des been thinking when he'd pulled her onto his lap and massaged her neck muscles, breathed in her ear?

"Ooh," she said aloud now, earning a quizzical look back at her from Ruffy. "Not you," she told her horse, then urged the animal into a slow canter. No, it was Des that brought up the "ooh" reaction, not to mention this funny hot little quivering sensation in the pit of her stomach that she hadn't experienced in years, if ever.

Lap-sitting, massaging, these were the actions of a man interested in a woman, weren't they? But they were also the way two good friends might interact with each other. She wasn't certain of that, of course, because Des was her first male friend so she didn't have a lot of experience with this kind of thing.

She'd seen her brother get physical with women who were friends, not lovers. Seen Didi hug all kinds of men she wasn't dating. The two of them had gone out for a drink one evening, after hitting the slots in a small nearby club, and Didi had perched on the lap of one of the regulars at the bar—a man who was happily married to Didi's childhood friend. There'd been nothing sexual about it, from what Gerri could tell, just friends kidding around.

She urged Ruffy into a gallop now, felt the wind in her hair and the rising sun on her face, tried to let her mind drift to topics other than Des and her. But, no, her mind rebelled against going into drift mode.

Hadn't Des asked her to spend his birthday with him, and didn't that mean he was interested in her as more than a friend? And weren't some of her mental and bodily reactions to him more than simply platonic?

She felt completely out of her element here. Quivers and doubts, doubts and quivers. Her male/female antennae were broken, and she knew it. She couldn't trust her instincts because they'd failed her in the past. And apart from the occasional date, she'd had very little practice since.

She tried to concentrate on the scenery, which was truly lovely. Joshua trees and sagebrush, snowcapped mountains and new spring blooms. A clear, cloudless morning sky, the hum of insects in the air.

But Des zoomed into her brain again. That final aside of his as he was leaving her shop last night, assuring her that at his birthday dinner on Friday night, they would be discussing business, her publishing his poetry. "Just friends," he'd been quick to assure her after asking her to join him.

Weren't expressions like "just friends" and "business" a kind of don't-get-interested-in-me-because-I'm-not-interested-in-you code? Darn, but she wished there was a handbook for this kind of situation. And oh, how she wished she had more experience in the world of dating.

On and on she rode, not able to take in any of the natural beauty around her, until she realized it was time to get back. She turned Ruffy around and headed back for Des's ranch.

If, as Gerri suspected, her feelings toward Des were morphing to something richer and deeper, wasn't that just perfect. Dandy. Once again, she was beginning to care for someone who only wanted her for what she could do for him.

Business-just friends-business-just friends. The phrases became a litany of dashed dreams as she rode. Really, she ought to stick to selling books and leave romance to the experts.

THURSDAY: Des caught up to Gerri near their frequent meeting place, the cottonwood grove. She'd loosened the reins so Ruffy could graze a bit, and was staring into the distance, a dreamlike expression on her face. She didn't even seem aware of his approach until he was right next to her. Then she shook herself and smiled that big welcoming grin of hers. It filled his chest cavity like warm milk.

"Des," she said, "I'm so glad to see you."

It was genuine, he was relieved to observe. She really was glad to see him.

He'd had his doubts when he'd hauled himself out of bed this morning, after the second of two sleepless nights. But he knew he couldn't avoid Gerri anymore.

Two nights earlier, he'd lowered his mask in front of her, revealed his secret writing in public and let her know of his interest in her personally. Chance-taking from a man who rarely indulged.

She'd been enthusiastic about the poetry, but, as for any interest in him, she'd seemed... *un*enthusiastic, to say the least. She'd stiffened when he got physical and hadn't leaped with joy when he'd asked her to dinner. How much more rejection could he—should he—take?

He understood that his pride was injured. He wasn't used to being rebuffed by women. Not that he'd had numerous conquests or considered himself irresistible, but he figured he was presentable, knew that when he was attracted to a woman she usually returned the attraction, and they went from there, most often to bed, which both of them enjoyed thoroughly. He also knew he was a considerate lover—he'd been told so, many times.

But his charm, what little he had, didn't seem to work with Gerri. There was some kind of push-pull thing going on. At one moment, he could swear she picked up on his interest in her, and returned it. In the next moment, she seemed disconcerted, her interest in him nowhere in evidence.

Was it him or her? Was it her inexperience or was he just not her type? Did she even have a type? Hell, did he? If he did, Gerri broke the mold.

Whatever. He had to get some sleep, which meant this had to be dealt with, one way or the other. He'd gotten out of bed with a purpose. Quickly he'd dressed, made coffee, went down to the stables and saddled Major. Avoidance wasn't getting him anywhere. If Gerri wasn't attracted to him, fine. Well, not *fine,* but he'd live through it.

Now, as he gazed on her fresh, open, morning face, he knew that he would hurt, and badly, if it didn't happen.

But, that smile of greeting dazzled him. Obviously she liked him, somewhat at least. And he was amazed at how much that fact meant to him. Damn. He was getting in deeper and deeper. Part of him was enjoying the sensation while the other part was sorry he'd ever met the woman at all.

"I'm glad to see you, too," he told her.

Then they both began talking at the same time: "I'm sorry if I seemed a little strange Tuesday night," Des said, just as Gerri chimed in with, "I wish you'd hung around on Tuesday night." They wound up in chorus on "Tuesday night," stopped together and laughed nervously. Then both of them said, "You first."

This time when they laughed, it was genuine.

"Ever been to the top of Geiger Peak?" Des said.

"No."

"Come."

With Major taking the lead, he led her along the banks of Steamboat Creek till they reached the foot of a long, high ridge of mountains. They embarked on a twisting, upward path, through dry trees and brush, Des making sure that none of the low-lying branches would catch Gerri by surprise. After about twenty minutes of constant climbing, they reached a section that flattened out before the trail upward began once again.

He led them onto the natural plateau and dismounted, then helped Gerri down, looping both of the horses' reins over a hedge. The ground was mostly dirt and pebbles, but a broad, flat rock sat perched at the edge of the outcropping, providing a handy bench on which to take advantage of the view.

"Go sit," he told Gerri. "I need to get something."

Her breath stopped at the beauty of the vista below them. Lit by the golden glow of first light, it went on for miles and miles of ranches and curving creeks. In the distance she could just make out the neon-lit casino buildings of downtown Reno. Even if, off to her right, the sun was beginning its daily climb upward, there were still pockets of darkness in the valleys below caused by the mountain range's shadows.

"Nice, huh," Des said from behind her.

"Astonishing," she said softly. A familiar smell assaulted her nostrils and she turned to see him holding a thermos and two sturdy cups.

"Coffee. Oh, Des, how perfect."

He sat next to her and poured her a steaming hot cup. "Hope you like it black."

"Absolutely." She sipped the brew, strong and heavenly, and they sat, side by side, for long silent minutes, staring out at the miracles below.

After a while, she turned to him and said simply, "Thank you."

He just nodded, a hint of a smile on his lips.

She studied his profile as he gazed over the panorama below. It was like something out of an Old West painting. Sturdy. Salt of the earth. Hard, even. His hat shaded his brow and halfway down his nose, perfectly imperfect with its slight bump near the bridge. The squint lines emanating from his eyes were deep, as were the creases in the rest of his face. Nice creases, she thought. 35-year-old creases. Des had a man's face, not a boy's.

Whatever she'd been feeling yesterday, this morning she felt safe, just being in his presence, drinking his coffee and soaking up the male strength of him.

Then he turned a morning-soft, blue-eyed gaze on her. "I wanted to show this to you because I knew you'd appreciate it."

Those eyes, she thought, struck by their mesmerizing color and expression. Whoever said blue eyes were cold was way off-base.

She inhaled deeply, taking in the fresh morning air, the hint of sagebrush, the strong coffee and Des's clean male sweat. "I do," she said softly. "Oh, yes, I do."

"I haven't brought anyone up here since—" He left the sentence unfinished, a frown creasing his brow.

"Since who?"

He paused before saying, "My wife. Ex-wife, actually."

"I didn't know you'd been married."

"It wasn't for long." He shrugged. "It's been over for years."

"Tell me about it," she coaxed, wondering if he would.

"Why?"

"Because you're still such a mystery to me. I feel like you know all about me, and I know practically nothing about you."

His chuckle was rueful. "You know all you need to know, believe me."

"Humor me."

She held her breath. He really was the most private man. But oh, how she wanted to know everything there was to know.

He gazed out again, his eyes squinting as the sun grew stronger. A flock of chattering birds flew overhead and he watched them as they faded into the distance. Then he began to speak. "Stella was a lounge singer at Harrah's. We married six weeks after we began dating. She told me she wanted to settle down, have kids, and I think she meant it at the time. But..."

He shrugged, like it was no big thing. "You know how those things go. We say a lot of things in the beginning we no longer mean at the end."

Wasn't that the truth, Gerri thought. "How long have you been divorced?"

"Over three years."

"Miss her?"

"Not in the least." Angling his head, he made eye contact with her, and she read the truth of the statement in his steady gaze. "Really. She's going after her dream, and more power to her."

She took another sip of coffee then pushed her luck. "And your family?"

"What about them?"

"Do you have brothers, sisters, parents?"

Shaking his head, Des chuckled softly. "Women,"

he said, "they always want to know all the background stuff."

"Only what you feel okay talking about."

He picked up a pebble from an indentation in the rock and threw it out over the vista below. She waited to see if he would go on, and was thankful when he did.

"I grew up in a small town in Montana. My dad was with the railroad and was gone a lot. My mother, well, she was…kind of fragile. She left me and my two brothers when I was eight—she couldn't take the old man's silences anymore. I don't remember her very well."

Gerri's eyes filled with tears for the child who'd been abandoned. "Oh Des, how awful."

"Hey, don't," he said, putting a broad hand on her arm, obviously uncomfortable with her compassion.

"Sorry." She swiped a thumb under her lower lids and told her tear ducts to cut it out. "Go on."

He removed his hand from her arm and picked up another pebble, studying it this time instead of throwing it. "We managed okay, except there was never enough money. I was the oldest. I quit school at sixteen and got a job on a ranch. I knew then I'd found what I wanted to do the rest of my life, so I saved my money and bought my spread and, well, that's the story."

"Where are they? Your brothers and your dad."

"The old man's gone, years ago. My brothers both went east. We talk on the phone once in a while, get together at Christmas. I'm an uncle four times now—two boys, two girls." The way he smiled at this last sentence let her know that having nieces and nephews pleased him.

It pleased her, too, to see this side of him. The side who wanted children of his own to share his home.

But he was so alone, and had been for a while. His aloneness had struck her from the beginning, and it hit her now like a sudden wave in a calm ocean. Again, she wanted to cry for him, but tamped down the urge before it became fact.

Des wondered why he wasn't bothered by Gerri's prying. He hated talking about himself—it seemed such a waste of time. But today, he was willing, which was just one more change going on internally, one of many changes that had begun with his decision to go public with his poetry.

Or had it begun when he met Gerri? He wasn't one to dwell on himself and his feelings, so he couldn't be sure.

But, here he was, as the expression went, "outed" at last, as a man with a sad past and future dreams. And he was deeply grateful it was Gerri sitting here to listen.

"I feel so lucky," she said, unconsciously echoing his own thoughts. He turned to gaze at her just as she sighed and peered off into the distance. "Both parents are still around and my brother's married but no kids yet—I've told you about them, I'm pretty sure. We're close, or rather we're closer now that I don't live near them anymore. Poor Mom and Dad. They never could quite figure out what to do with me."

"Because of your brain."

"No," she said easily and smiled at him. "We all have a lot of gray matter—it's in the genes, going way back, so I can't take credit for it. My dad's a professor at Columbia, my mom's a psychoanalyst. I was a computer nerd from early on, not very good socially, if you know what I mean. But, boy, could I do school.''

"You never mentioned where you went to college.''

She wrinkled her nose. "My turn to tell all, huh?''

"It's only fair.''

"Okay.'' She set her cup down next to her, then brought her knees to her chest and wrapped her arms around them. "I went to MIT at age sixteen, got my Ph.D. in computer science at twenty-two, was lucky enough to get involved with an up-and-coming dot com when they were still burning up the NASDAQ wires, got out before the crash, cashed in and, as they say, here I am. Now I only use my computer for business records and e-mail. I prefer real life to the one on the little screen. I'm a reformed techie and proud of it.''

He grinned in appreciation of her humor. "Why a bookstore in Nevada?''

"Because I've never felt as happy as I do in a bookstore. I've always been a voracious reader. You, too?''

When he nodded, she went on. "As for the Nevada part, well, I fell in love with horses at an early age, always wanted one of my own. And—promise you won't laugh—I have a secret addiction to the twenty-five cent blackjack machines. So, when I got a chance to buy the shop *and* have a horse, both of them in a state where gambling's legal, I mean—'' she opened her hands, palms up "—how could I pass it up?''

"Seems fated, for sure," he said with a chuckle. "What else do you want to know?"

"Ever been married?"

A beat went by before she said, "Hardly."

"In love?" When the smile left her face he felt like taking the question back.

"Once," she said before he could let her off the hook. "A long time ago. He broke my heart."

He said nothing, waiting for her to tell him more. She did, making a dismissive gesture with her hand. "Oh, it's so silly. His name was Tommy and he was quite a bit older than me. I was an eighteen-year-old college junior, flattered that a doctoral candidate was paying attention to me. We were together for a year, and then I found out that all he'd ever really wanted from me was help with his thesis. I practically wrote the whole thing for him. And then—" she shrugged "—he didn't need me anymore."

The protectiveness that rose in his chest took Des by surprise, and he knew if the guy were here, he'd pound him to a pulp. "What a creep."

"I agree. A major creep. And there's been nobody special since then," she said offhandedly, although he doubted she was as casual about it as she was trying to appear. "I guess that puts me in the once-burned-twice-shy category."

So, she wasn't a virgin, Des thought. But she might as well have been. If it had been ten years since she'd been involved, it had been ten years since she'd been to bed with anyone—he'd make book on it. Gerri would never take sex lightly. She wasn't the type.

"I guess I'm kind of a dork, huh," she said, turning toward him and resting her cheek on her knees.

"Not to me," he told her.

Out of nowhere, it struck Des that he and Gerri were never this close to each other, physically, when they had their conversations. They were always on horseback or saying hello and goodbye in passing.

Now, he was able to get a really thorough look at her face, and he found it... The word was one his mother used way back when she'd been home. *Dear.* Her hazel eyes were translucent in the rising dawn. That sprinkling of freckles across her nose and cheeks made her look fresh and innocent. Hers was a gentle, nice, *dear* face, beautiful in its way, although not classically so.

It was a face he could look at and never get tired of.

"No, you're not a dork," he murmured again, moving a little closer to her. "I think you just..." He sought the right words. "I think you feel things deeply and so you're, well, cautious. Anyway, your life isn't over. You're still pretty young."

"Getting less so each day," she observed wryly.

He reached over to stroke her upturned cheek. Petal soft, as he'd known it would be. Startled, she raised her head at his touch, but didn't pull away, so he cupped her chin with both hands, leaned in and kissed her, gently. A hello kiss, not impassioned, but not disinterested, either.

As Des rubbed his soft lips over hers, Gerri closed her eyes and found herself welcoming his kiss eagerly. Heat rose from the bottom of her toes and spread throughout the rest of her body. Unfurling her arms from around her knees, she rested one hand on the rock next to her and angled her body closer to

Des's, leaning in for more. He gave her more, by thrusting his tongue into her mouth, and she welcomed it with her own. Time stopped as she drank him in like water after a drought.

When she heard a satisfied humming noise, and realized it was coming from the back of her throat, she withdrew quickly, embarrassed. Thoroughly flustered, she bent her head to study her lap.

"You have the softest mouth," Des murmured, nuzzling the area of her neck behind her ear.

"So do you," she admitted, her breath hitching as her body continued to respond to his touch.

"Why did you pull away?"

"I...wasn't sure what to do next."

He placed a finger under her chin and raised her head so she could meet his gaze. "There's nothing *to* do. That was just a kiss, Gerri," he said, his eyes serious. "Nothing more will happen until or unless you want it to."

Her treacherous face heated up as she confessed, "I guess I...want it to."

One side of his mouth quirked up. "Glad to hear it."

"And I'm scared to death."

God, Des thought, how could one woman allow herself to be so unguarded, so lacking in protection? He drew in a deep breath then let it out. "Why don't we talk about it some more tomorrow night?"

"Tomorrow night?" Her eyes were unfocused.

"My birthday."

"Oh, right." She shook her head as though trying to reassemble scrambled brains. "Yes, of course.

Your birthday.'' She frowned suddenly as a thought seemed to occur to her.

"Are we still on?"

"Yes. Of course." He waited for her to continue, but she didn't seem about to. There'd been enough questions and answers between them today.

"Good." He rose and offered his hand, then pulled her up. "Come. We both have to get back to real life."

The ride down the mountainside was peaceful, which matched the relative calm Des felt inside. His exhaustion was gone, and life looked a lot better now.

Rance was history. Gerri was his. He'd known it the minute they'd kissed. It would take a while, kind of like taming a terrified mare, but he would earn her trust. He understood now what made her tick, understood what she needed.

All day, Gerri found her fingers touching her mouth, which she could swear continued to vibrate from Des's kiss. She was distracted, and that wouldn't do, as Cassie Nevins was coming to the store for a book-signing, and Gerri was expecting a crowd.

Had the morning been as magical as it had seemed? Had she and Des really confided in each other, let each other in on early hurts? Had there been a kind of communion between them, real intimacy, for the first time?

Had he really kissed her as though she were an attractive and desirable woman? Had he promised more, if she wanted it?

And had she really told him she wanted it?

Oh, God, how blatant could you get? Had she appeared totally out of it, as uncool as it was possible to be? If she had, he hadn't seemed to mind.

More would be revealed, she thought with simmering excitement as she set up the folding chairs for the book-signing. Lots and lots more. Her lips quivered again. She could hardly wait.

As Cassie was packing up her carrying case with leftover bookmarks, stickers and pens, she called over to Gerri, who was cleaning up the refreshment area. "Thanks again, Gerri, for a wonderful event."

"My pleasure, needless to say. Oh, before you go, I need to ask you something."

The store was empty for the moment, thank heavens, so Gerri walked over to the author and asked, "Remember those glasses you gave me? The turquoise ones?"

"Of course," Cassie said with a broad smile. "How could I forget them? Have you made your wish yet?"

Gerri looked around the room again, just in case someone was there she didn't know about. This was private stuff. But no, there were no customers at the moment. "I sure have," she said, pulling a chair over to the table, "and I'm kind of confused."

"Tell me." Cassie closed her case and turned to face her. "I want to hear, all of it."

Relieved that she could finally unburden herself about "the wish" and not be laughed at, she did just that, told her the whole story, how it had been before and how it was this week. And how confused she felt about her feelings for Des, and what was she to do the next night, if and when Rance asked her to the fund-raiser?

"Wow," Cassie said when the tale was told, "you really got your wish, didn't you?"

"Did I?"

"Sounds like it. You wanted to do the week over, and do it right, isn't that what you wished for?"

"Yes. But I'm so confused. I hoped you'd have some answers."

"What kind of answers?"

Gerri sat, glumly, her elbow on the table, her chin in her hand. After a few moments, she asked, "Did your wish come true?"

"Yes. I asked for someone to rescue my daughter and me. And someone did."

"Was he the man you'd been waiting for all your life?"

Cassie's smile was sad, her look faraway. "To some extent, yes. But...he couldn't stay."

"Oh. So, the wish was a bust."

"Not in the least. I didn't get the man I thought I wanted, but I sure got the one I needed."

"Excuse me?"

The author covered Gerri's hand with her own and squeezed it. "I got the man of my dreams, believe me. Just not quite in the way I'd expected."

"Oh. Hmm. I don't understand," Gerri admitted finally, "but then I guess I'm not supposed to." While Cassie looked on sympathetically, Gerri sighed deeply. "I don't know what to do about tomorrow night."

"I wish I could help. It sounds like the only thing

you can do, and this will sound corny, is to follow your heart, wherever it leads you.''

"Will it lead me to Rance or Des?'' It was a rhetorical question, and both of them knew it.

Cassie shrugged. "The glasses are magic, but I'm sure not,'' she said ruefully. Again, she patted Gerri's hand, then rose. "Don't be scared. Trust. I'm sure the right answer will come when it's needed.''

FRIDAY: By late afternoon, Gerri's stomach was in knots as she stood behind the cash register, thrumming her fingers on the countertop. Although why, she wasn't sure. She'd made her decision: she was going out to dinner with Des, as she'd promised. He'd asked first, so there really was no discussion needed.

And she couldn't wait to be with him tonight, most especially after that kiss. Heck, she was downright eager.

It was just that, having made "the wish,'' she'd expected to attend the fund-raiser. With Rance. Looking elegant and desirable. Wasn't that the purpose of the whole wish thing, for heaven's sake? How would she feel if she never got to see that through?

But there was Des and her burgeoning feelings for him. Did it really matter if she didn't see "the wish'' through?

The bell went off as the door opened; at the same moment, the phone rang. Torn from her mental meanderings, Gerri glanced over to see who had come in. Des stood in the doorway, and the quiver became more of a flutter that took wing and filled her with happiness. As she stared at him, she was vaguely aware that someone else had picked up the phone.

She had this insane urge to run up to him and throw her arms around him, but there were people in the shop. Besides, she sternly reminded herself, nothing had happened between them but a kiss. She couldn't act in public as though the two of them were an item, as if there were something significant between them—even if she hoped there would be, eventually—because that wasn't the truth.

Not yet.

"Hi," he said, smiling that half smile of his as he walked toward her. Under his arm he held a thick manila envelope which he set down on the counter in front of her.

"Hi," she said shyly.

"I brought you these. My poems." He was self-conscious, she could tell. "I, uh, well, I thought you might want to look them over before I pick you up tonight."

"Oh, Des, I'd love to. Happy birthday, by the way."

"I hope you'll say that with a little more enthusiasm later." The words were innocent, but the slyly suggestive look in his eye would have melted a statue.

"I'll work on my delivery," she countered, her stomach doing somersaults of happiness as she did.

She barely heard the bell as the door opened one more time.

"Gerri?" The voice was male and petulant.

Both she and Des turned to look at the newcomer. It was Rance.

Chapter Six

Instinctively Gerri glanced at the clock on the wall behind her: 5:45 p.m. This, at least, was the same as last week; it was at precisely that time that Rance had strode into the shop, oblivious of everything and everyone around him, complaining loudly as he headed toward Gerri, exactly as he was doing now.

It looked as though history—in this case, at least—was about to repeat itself.

"My mother has got to be stopped, Gerri, seriously," he said, gripping the edge of the counter and earnestly talking to her. "I really can't take it anymore. If she doesn't end this stupid matchmaking, I'm going to move to another city. That'll show her."

With a scowl of disgust, he began to pace, walking a few steps to the end of the counter and back to where she stood, in the center at the cash register. He seemed to have no idea that Des was also present, his mouth turned down in a frown as he watched him.

Last week, before "the wish," Gerri had been on the phone with a customer, chatting about the new Barbara Kingsolver. At Rance's appearance, she'd excused herself, hung up and asked Rance what had happened.

Today, however, Des had shown up, so an assistant had taken care of the phone. Gerri remembered what she'd said to Rance last week: "What on earth has happened? Tell me all about it."

Today she rebelled against following a script. This was her wish, darn it, so instead of pursuing Rance's problems, she said, "Rance, do you know Des Quinlan?"

The blond man paused in his pacing to absentmindedly gaze in Des's direction. "Hmm? Oh, yeah, sure," he said, offering his hand. "We've met a few times. How're you doing?"

"I'm all right," Des answered, returning the handshake stone-faced.

"Bunny Reagan," Rance said to Gerri, dropping Des's hand and dismissing him in an instant. "Can you believe it? She wants me to ask Bunny Reagan out."

"I have no idea who you're talking about."

"She's my mother's oldest friend's goddaughter, thirty years old, never been married, but really wants children, I'm told. She's some kind of scientist, I don't know, she studies ancient insect corpses or something like that. When I asked Mother what she looked like, she told me looks weren't important, character was. Can you believe that?"

He looked at her for commiseration, but didn't wait to get it. "Earlier in the day—" he resumed his pacing "—she'd taken a couple of pot shots at Marla, saying that women who had breast enhancements usually couldn't nurse their children, and that the first six months of breast milk were really crucial to a child's health and well-being."

Gerri bit back a smile, as she had last week. Back then, she'd never met Rance's mother, but was favorably inclined to like her. "What did Marla say?"

"That she completely agreed and was really grateful her entire body was God's creation. I saw Mother winding up for a zinger, so I said goodbye, grabbed Marla by the hand and got us out of there."

"Poor Rance." Gerri glanced over at Des to see if he was as amused by the story as she was, but his expression hadn't changed a bit. His mouth was still set in a firm, disapproving line. She suddenly remembered that Des didn't like Rance. They'd discussed him on the phone just the other night.

Uh-oh, she thought, sensing Des's disapproval. *I hope this is over soon.*

Rance was still complaining, still walking back and forth. "Why do I put up with this, Gerri, tell me?"

"Because she's your mother and you love her? What do you think, Des?" She turned to him with a bright smile.

Des cleared his throat, then shifted his attention away from Rance to face her. "Listen," he said, not responding to her question, "about tonight—"

"Yes, Des, let's talk about tonight," she said encouragingly, still smiling at him and pointedly ignoring Rance. This would most probably annoy the other man. But, it served him right.

It was unforgivable how Rance always demanded

to be the center of attention. She'd never noticed before how selfish he was that way—dismissing anyone who wasn't of use to him, going on and on about himself and rarely asking others about themselves or sticking around long enough to listen.

She'd been enthralled with what she perceived as superb social skills and enormous self-confidence, but what he was, really, was totally self-absorbed. His manner could be hypnotic, that was for sure, but she didn't have to fall under his spell.

Rance had yet to get that Gerri and Des had changed the subject. "Damn that Marla for putting me in this situation. If she hadn't had to be in Montreal on a shoot at five in the morning, she could have taken a later plane. But, no, she had to screw up my whole evening, and I had to listen to Mother suggesting alternate dates."

"Dates for what?" It was out of her mouth before she could stop it—the same question Gerri had asked Rance last week. But she'd intended to pay attention to Des and ignore Rance. What had happened?

"This big fund-raiser," Rance answered, shaking his head in disgust. "It's this charity event and it's tonight. I have to show up—my family is on the board."

"Tonight?"

Like some sort of automaton, she was keeping to the script, couldn't seem to help herself. Her gaze left Des and now followed Rance as he continued his back and forth pacing. She was aware of Des, but couldn't tear her gaze away from the other man.

"Yeah, it's for some childhood disease my mother

feels strongly about, and now I don't have a date. Damn that Marla.''

Suddenly he stopped, the look on his face one of intense concentration as inspiration seemed to hit him. Slowly he looked over at Gerri. She watched the idea take shape, knew before he opened his mouth what he was about to say.

No, she wanted to cry out. *No, don't say it.*

"You." He banged a clenched fist on the counter for emphasis. "Gerri, you could do it!"

"Do what?"

"Be my date for this thing tonight." Leaning his elbows on the countertop, he clasped his hands in the classic pose of supplication. "I'll be forever grateful."

"Me?"

"Yes, of course you. Throw on an evening gown and some makeup and you'll be fine. Nothing like Marla, all flash. No, you'll be—" he stood back, checked her out as one would a painting he was considering buying "—serious looking. Yes. This way I won't have to go out with Bunny whatever-her-name-is. And I won't have to fight off all the single women and their mothers, who take one look at an eligible bachelor and swoop down on him like…like—"

"Pigeons to bread crumbs?" Gerri supplied, on cue.

Rance snapped his fingers. "Yes. That's it exactly. Instead I'll show up with you."

"I can't, Rance." She'd said that last week, too, but then it had been because of how flustered and flattered and scared she'd felt at his invitation. Back then—it was painfully obvious to her now—she hadn't allowed herself to hear the condescension behind the invitation.

"Of course you can!" he insisted. "What do you need? A dress? You can leave early, can't you? Go buy a gown? All the casinos have dress shops."

Des felt a slow, simmering rage rising in him like a long-dormant volcano. This guy was incredible. A steamroller, a narcissist, a total jerk.

And Gerri was paying him attention, going along with him. Why?

He could only come up with two answers. Either she was being polite to Rance, or she still had a thing for him. He hated the second one, but forced himself to face facts. If, despite what they'd shared yesterday morning, Gerri still had that crush on Golden Boy and wanted a chance to move it along, this invitation was the perfect opportunity. Hell, it was a dream come true.

He studied her reaction, but it was difficult to read her. Was she going to do it or wasn't she? Out of nowhere, she shot him a look that was pure panic.

Panic? Why? He didn't understand her, dammit. Did she or did she not want to go to the stupid fundraiser with Rance? And more important to Des, did she or did she not want to have dinner with him, instead? As had already been arranged, already agreed on.

Tell him, he willed her, seething inside. *Tell this moron you can't go out with him tonight because you have a previous commitment. You're previously committed to going out with me.*

But, nothing from Gerri, because good ol' Rance was still talking, still doing his sales job, as he unfolded a huge wad of money. "I'll pay for the dress. Here." He peeled off several bills and handed them to her.

"Put that back," Gerri told him, pushing his hand away. "I can buy my own dress, thank you."

Des waited for the follow-up, something about how she didn't need his damned money or a new dress, as she wasn't going anywhere with him. She was going out with Des to celebrate his birthday.

But the moment passed, and Gerri didn't follow up, and slowly, something small and hopeful that had begun to blossom inside him, died a little.

He watched Rance flash her that cocky grin. "Okay, okay, I can't buy you off. Does that mean you'll go? You'd save my butt big-time if you do. Say yes, Gerri."

Say no, Gerri, Des said silently.

And, as though she'd heard him, she shook her head. "I can't, Rance. Sorry, but I'm—"

She never finished the sentence because the door burst open and a short, round, pretty woman came barreling through it like a ball of sheer energy. "Hey, Gerri! How's it go—?"

Oh, no. Gerri's eyes widened at Didi's lively entrance, not sure whether help had arrived or yet one more distraction. The tableau facing her made Didi stop dead in her tracks, and Gerri could just imagine what she was seeing: Gerri behind the counter, her fingers clutching the edge with tension, Des and Rance on either side of her, both looking at her, Rance with his hands clasped before him in prayer, Des, glowering, with *his* hands in fists at his side.

With a weak wave, Gerri said, "Hi, Didi."

Didi's gaze went from her to Rance to Des and back to her again. "Hi back," she said, her eyes telegraphing a "What gives?" message.

"Didi, you know Rance, right?" When her friend nodded, she indicated Des. "I don't think you've ever met Des Quinlan?"

"No, I don't think so," Didi said, smiling at him and not masking the female appreciation in her gaze. "Hi."

"Des owns the ranch where I board Ruffy," Gerri added brightly.

"Oh, yeah, right. Listen, I seem to have interrupted something. What I wanted to know was, uh, well, actually it looks like you *will* be, or rather, will you be needing me after all, for, you know," she said, "that *thing* we discussed? At the mall?"

"Actually," Gerri began, but Rance hastened over to Didi, grabbed her hand and pulled her toward the counter.

"Didi," he said forcefully, "you're just in time. Help me convince Gerri to be my date tonight for this stupid fund-raiser. I have to go, and she has to go with me. It starts in a little over two hours. It's life and death to me."

Withdrawing her hand from Rance's grasp, Didi observed sardonically, "Aren't you being a tad dramatic?"

He had the grace to grin back. "Hey, I'm a desperate man. I'll try anything."

Didi looked at Gerri, her gaze again saying "What's happening here?" as she said, "So? It's a free meal and dancing. And you have that new dress,'' she added pointedly. "Why not go with the guy?"

Gerri glanced quickly at Des, who hadn't been heard from in a while, then back again to her friend. "Thanks for the opinion, Didi, but I don't think I can—"

"Sure," Des said abruptly, "why not go with the guy." It was not a question but a statement.

Gerri turned to him in dismay. "What?"

Des shrugged, his face totally devoid of expression. "What the hell, we can have dinner another time."

Even as Gerri was feeling as though Des had stabbed her with a knife, the light seemed to dawn for Rance. "Is that the problem? That you were supposed to go out to dinner with Des tonight?" Eagerly he peeled off a few more bills. "Well then, let me buy you two dinner. Just not tonight. Tomorrow, okay?" He held out the bills, offering them first to one, then the other, confident now. "One more night won't make a difference, will it?"

Again, Des shrugged, but didn't take the money. "No, it won't. We were just going to discuss some business, anyway, right, Gerri?"

"Were we?" She knew the hurt must have showed on her face but she couldn't help it.

"Weren't we?" he countered enigmatically, and she understood that she was supposed to say or do something now to make everything all right.

"But—" she laid a tentative hand on his arm "—it's your birthday."

"Really?" Rance chimed in enthusiastically. "Happy birthday. But, you can celebrate it tomorrow night just as well as tonight, right?"

Des was on the verge of turning to the man and ramming a fist down his throat, but he exerted all the restraint he could muster to keep himself from losing it. He would not show how much he cared, how much he was hurting, not in front of anyone, especially not in front of Gerri.

If she'd wanted to be with him this evening, she'd have made it clear to Rance immediately, and by now, the discussion would have been long over. But, from the beginning, she'd waffled. *See?* that voice inside of him said. *You can't trust women. They leave when they get a better offer. That's how they are and how they always will be.*

He was aware that his tendency to paint an entire sex with one paintbrush might not be fair, but dammit, at this very moment, it was hard to ignore the evidence right in front of him.

"Put your money away," he said gruffly to Rance who, realizing he was still holding out the bills and no one was taking them, shrugged and returned them to his pocket.

"Whatever the man says," Rance said cheerfully. "After all, it's his birthday."

"That's right. We can celebrate my birthday tomorrow night, right, Gerri? Or next week," he said offhandedly. "Or never."

Damn. He hated that he'd said that last bit out loud instead of keeping his mouth shut. It showed he was wounded, that he cared too much. Thoroughly disgusted with himself, and with Rance and Gerri and just about the entire world, he turned on his heel and headed for the exit.

Gerri ran around the counter and caught up to him

as he yanked the door open. "Des," she cried, grabbing his elbow. "Are you sure?"

He held himself stiffly, afraid if he turned to look at her, he'd lose it completely. "Yeah, no problem," he muttered, then began to walk out.

"But I thought—" From behind him, her voice was small and hurt-sounding.

Gritting his teeth, he forced himself to face her. "Yeah?" he said, propping a shoulder against the doorjamb. "What did you think?"

Gerri took an involuntary step backward at the expression on Des's face. Icy and remote, this was the look of a man who didn't care about her, or about anything. Gone was the open, laughing Des, gone was the subtle flirtation of just moments before, the unscripted moments before Rance walked through the doorway, as he'd been destined to do.

She forced herself to gaze into Des's eyes and for a moment, she imagined she saw a small flicker of wounded pride in their depths. But in the next instant, whatever she'd seen—or imagined—was gone, and now she faced a pair of cold blue stones.

One more attempt to make contact, she told herself. She owed both of them that. Rubbing her hands together nervously, she gazed at him, pleading silently to let her in. "I guess I thought—" She stopped herself, because if anything, his expression got harder, more remote.

"Yes? What did you think?"

"Something completely off base, I guess," she finished weakly.

A muscle in his jaw clenched once, then once

more. Without another word, he turned and was gone, leaving her to gaze after him, totally deflated.

Needless to say, her mind was racing back and forth, trying to make sense of what had just occurred here.

She'd been positive there was something special developing between her and Des, even if their date this evening had been set up only after she'd offered to publish his poetry.

But what was she to think now? Had their kiss been a thank-you and nothing more? His attitude tonight seemed to indicate that. Go with Rance, he'd said.

No, she told herself. Something was wrong. Even if she was hopeless at understanding men, she trusted her instincts about people in general, and there was some war going on inside Des that he wasn't letting her in on. Why? And what?

Was it possible he was using her, the way Tommy had? She didn't want to believe it, didn't believe it, in truth.

But he was gone now.

Rance was here, though, present and accounted for, faithfully enacting his role in "the wish." And, in his favor, at least he was being up-front about the fact that he wanted to use her. She would save him from his mother and her matchmaking friends. Sure, he'd invited her out, but it wasn't personal. Last week, she hadn't wanted to know that; this week, she got it, loud and clear.

Des didn't want her, either, it seemed. Which meant she was, as they said, batting 0 for 2 in the romance department.

But then, she thought with uncharacteristic bitterness, why should this day be different from any other?

She turned away from the door and looked over at Rance and Didi, both watching her with questions in their eyes. Back to the present, Gerri ordered herself. Back to the finale of "the wish": To go to the fundraiser tonight and do it right this time.

Really, now that Des was gone, there was no decision left to make, was there?

She walked over to Rance, and with a small smile said, "Sure, I'll go with you."

It wasn't a very enthusiastic response, but he didn't seem to care. He gave her two thumbs-up. "Terrific. I'll pick you up at eight, okay?" He headed for the door, calling over his shoulder, "Gerri, I won't forget this, really."

"Rance?"

He stopped in his tracks, turned. "Yes?"

"You might want to know my address."

"Oh, yeah, sure." He chuckled as he walked back to the counter. While Gerri was writing the information on a pad, he glanced at Didi. "So, how's everything with you?" he said, obviously just passing the time.

"Just dandy," Didi said. Gerri was pretty sure Rance missed the sarcasm.

After she handed him the piece of paper, he took off. Gerri looked at Didi, who opened her mouth to speak. But, once again, they were interrupted. Whoever was in charge of timing had a wicked sense of humor.

"Miss?" A customer with a stack of paperbacks came up to the counter. "May I buy these, please?"

"Sure," Gerri said with automatic cheer that didn't make it to her insides.

As she rang up the sale, she couldn't help comparing how it had been last week at the same moment. Then, having said yes to Rance and having given him her address and waved goodbye, she'd been so excited she hadn't been sure her small chest cavity could contain her expanding heart.

Rance had asked her out! Sure it was last minute, she'd told herself, and sure it had nothing to do with her beauty or lack thereof. But maybe they could get to know each other better and he would see her for who she really was. She would meet his mother and probably the rest of his family, and maybe they would like her.

Last week, the prospect of the evening ahead had been an occasion for great joy.

This week, it just wasn't that big a deal. All she could wonder about was what had happened with Des? What had changed? Had she done or said something to offend him? Or had she just read more into a nice conversation and one kiss than either merited?

Didi waited patiently for Gerri to finish up with her customer before she spoke again. "Are you going to tell me what just went on here?"

"Don't," Gerri said, then busied herself closing out her drawer. If she was going to get ready, she needed to leave now. "Melissa," she called to her assistant, "I have to take off early. Will you please take over?"

Didi rested her elbows on the counter and said softly, "Hey, *amiga,* you look like someone just took your best doll and threw it in the river."

Her friend's sympathy made her feel even worse. She shook her head. "If I live to be a hundred I will never understand what makes the male mind tick."

"Don't try, it's a lost cause. So, Rance actually asked you out, just like you said he would. Wow, do I believe in magic now, or what?" She grinned, then noticed that Gerri wasn't smiling back. "Okay now, give. Who is this Des hunk, what is he to you and what are you to him?"

"Apparently not much," Gerri said with a sigh. "It's a long story. Listen, are you still willing to meet me at my house and turn me into something approaching presentable?"

"So long as I get to hear the whole long story. Go home and wash your hair. I'll be there in twenty minutes."

Chapter Seven

Des stood in the doorway of the hardware store and watched as Gerri and her friend came out of her bookstore, laughing about something, then waved goodbye to each other. Gerri disappeared down the driveway in the middle of the block and returned in a few minutes behind the wheel of her car.

It took him a moment to hop into his truck, which was parked nearby, and follow her. He wasn't quite sure why he had to do this, something about wanting to know where she lived. He had her address, but it was back at the ranch and he needed to know now.

He kept several cars between them and almost lost her when she turned up a narrow road cut into the mountainside. By the time he caught up to her, she was walking into her house, a Victorian-era two-story structure that she'd obviously put some money into. He sat in his car, fidgety and out of sorts.

Maybe he ought to go in, straighten out whatever

needed to be straightened out. But what had happened between them was all murky to him.

He couldn't shake the feeling that he'd behaved badly with Gerri, set her up to fail in some way, but didn't seem able to get a handle on it. All he was sure of was that she was supposed to be with him tonight; instead she was going to some formal affair with Rance. Des would be alone.

A wave of self-pity threatened, but he hated self-pity and told himself to get a grip. Okay, so it was his birthday—he didn't have to spend it alone. He could go where there was lots of noise, lots of other people. He put the truck into Reverse. He would return to town, get a drink or three. After all, birthdays were for celebrating.

Gerri gazed at her reflection in the antique, three-paneled mirror, took in the wet stringy hair, pale skin, the barest suggestion of curves where most women had real in-and-out contours, and sighed loudly.

Hopeless, that's what she was. Utterly hopeless.

She removed the black dress from its plastic cover, hung it over one of the panels and studied it. The garment was lovely, but it wasn't really her, and she knew it. It was way more sophisticated than she could pull off. Still, at least she wouldn't look like a ruffled nightmare this evening, as she had last time.

Didi rang the bell and Gerri threw on a robe and ran downstairs to answer the door. Her friend entered, loaded down with bags and packages and something in a huge garment bag slung over her shoulder.

"What is this?" Gerri asked, taking several of the bundles in her arms.

"A surprise. Let's get going."

As Didi headed for the stairs, Gerri trailed after her. "It's hopeless, you know."

"Nonsense," Didi threw over her shoulder.

But no, it wasn't nonsense. Gerri had looked in the mirror and she knew.

Des caught his reflection in the mirrored wall behind the bar, and what he saw wasn't pretty. He was glowering, the expression on his face mean and ornery.

Here he was, as intended, in the bar of a big casino. There were people and noise. Just what he'd wanted. He'd had one drink and was on his second. As he signaled the bartender for a third, he wondered if that was a smart move. His dad used to come home from working on the railroad, sit at the kitchen table, and really tie one on. Des and his brothers had known not to get near the old man at those times because he tended to get violent.

Des didn't want to turn into his father. In fact, he'd never been much of a drinker. But it was his birthday, dammit, and he wanted to celebrate in some way.

A woman's high-pitched laughter rang out near him. Yes, that was what he needed. A woman.

Turning on his stool, he gazed around the huge bar area and saw a couple of possibilities—a blonde over in the corner seated alone at a table, a redhead a little ways down the bar. He realized he'd seen the redhead earlier, in the mirror, not-too-subtly staring at him. When he nodded at her she smiled, raised her glass to him and drank.

He picked up what was left of his scotch and ambled over to join her.

"Wow!"

Gerri stood in front of her mirror again, but this time she couldn't believe the vision that stared out at her. The transformation had taken nearly two hours—during which she'd told Didi the details of what had gone on with her and Des all week—and in that time, Didi had done wonders with her hair. It was swept up off her face, with soft curls piled high and tiny pearls scattered throughout them.

The makeup was even more of a miracle. Her eyes looked huge, her cheekbones prominent, her mouth inviting. She looked…elegant.

Now she stood in a strapless bra and slip and watched while Didi—who had told her to hang the black number back in the closet—opened up the garment bag and removed a long, cream-colored gown of a soft silky material.

"That's the one in your shop window," Gerri gasped. "It's an antique."

"Uh-huh. Do you like it?"

"Like it? I love it! I've been admiring it for months."

"Well, tonight, it's yours."

Gerri's hand flew to her chest. "But, I couldn't."

"You could, and will."

"But it's valuable."

"Which is why it's insured. Put it on."

Even as Didi was slipping the dress over her head, Gerri kept protesting. "But Didi—"

"Stop 'but'-ing me."

Gerri let the dress fall around her, then turned to watch as Didi fastened up the hooks in the back.

"Oh my," she said, staring wide-eyed at the woman in the mirror.

The dress was fashioned in the empire style, worn off the shoulder, its neckline cut low enough to expose just the tops of her breasts. Its waistline was high and fitted under the bustline. The rest of the soft, filmy fabric fell straight from there, nearly to the floor. The sleeves were short and puffed, and the entire dress had tiny seed pearls scattered all over it.

"Oh my," she said again, as Didi stood behind and to the right of her, both of them checking out the mirror's reflection.

"'Oh my' indeed," Didi replied smugly. "Exactly as I thought. You, my dear friend, are a knockout."

The off-the-shoulder styling made her too-long neck seem graceful and refined. Her height made the dress fall just right, hinting at long, slender legs beneath the skirt. She even had a little cleavage! Just a hint, just enough.

"It's beautiful," Gerri whispered. "But it isn't me."

"Then who else is that we're looking at?" When Gerri didn't answer, Didi stated, "No more, okay? Now for the finishing touch."

Didi reached into one of her bags and withdrew an antique diamond-and-pearl choker, matching bracelet and long white gloves. Feeling as though she were starring in her own dream, Gerri dutifully added these last pieces to her ensemble.

Just then the doorbell rang. Automatically Gerri

turned away from the mirror to get it, but Didi put up a staying hand. "I'll go."

While her friend ran downstairs to greet Rance, she quickly slipped into her sandals, transferred what she needed from her purse to a little silver clutch, then checked her reflection one more time in the mirror.

A princess, she thought. This was exactly what she'd prayed for, wished for, not merely last week, but all her life. And in just a few moments, the rest of her wish would be acted out—she would go to the ball, on Rance's arm.

She frowned, her reverie interrupted by the realization that, as the week had unfurled, it had been Des she'd been yearning for, not Rance.

No, she told herself firmly, no more thoughts of Des. He'd brushed her off, handed her to Rance. Why, she didn't know, but she guessed it was because he had what the women's magazines called baggage. After their talk yesterday, she now had a hint of what that baggage was.

But that was no excuse for his attitude two hours ago, she told herself with a small spurt of temper. He'd been cold to her, hurt her.

"Well, too bad," she told her reflection. "Just too darn bad for you, Des." Just as suddenly as it had risen, the anger at Des dissipated. "Oh, Des," she moaned. "Why aren't I spending your birthday with you?"

It was with a heavy heart that she turned away from the mirror, opened the bedroom door, and prepared to meet the ex man of her dreams.

At the top of the stairs, she paused one last time, warning herself to be really careful as she descended them. If she tripped right now, she'd have to find a cave to live in for the rest of her natural life.

But she didn't trip, she *floated* down the stairs and into the foyer, where Rance stood conversing with Didi while peering into the hallway mirror and raking his fingers through his already perfect hair.

"Good evening," Gerri said, and it felt as though someone else were speaking. She sounded calmly self-possessed, as though she wore gowns and diamonds every day.

Rance turned from his own reflection and, she had to admit it, got the reaction she'd dreamed of since she was an awkward, too-tall child.

His mouth dropped. Literally dropped and would have fallen to the floor had it not been attached to his jawline.

"Gerri," Rance said softly. "You look... beautiful."

Not really, she wanted to say. It's the dress and the makeup, it's all an illusion. But she didn't, because she knew just what was expected of her. "Thank you. You look great in a tux. Shall we go?"

Who was this woman, Gerri wondered silently, and why was she saying these totally appropriate things? Where was the old Gerri, pooh-poohing all compliments, too eager to put herself down, too willing to take responsibility for any awkward moment or hurt feelings?

Gone. For tonight, at least. The wish had been to redo the past week, and the week would be over in about three hours. Three more hours of magic time.

Well then, she told herself, damn the torpedoes and full speed ahead!

*   *   *

The redhead had been only too pleased to talk about herself. Two divorces, no kids. She was a top-less dancer in one of the casino shows, and had the right body for it; tonight she wore a tight V-neck sweater over tighter leather pants and high heels. Early to mid-thirties, he figured, with the beginnings of lines of desperation around her eyes. Since they'd been talking she'd issued lots of hints that she wouldn't mind if they blew this joint and let nature take its course.

But he wasn't moving toward that goal. Couldn't, really. It wasn't the fact that he'd had four drinks and was sipping his fifth. It wasn't the fact that he didn't find her attractive because he did, in a kind of one-night stand way. It wasn't even that he didn't feel himself up to the task, so to speak, because liquor had never affected his abilities that way.

No, it was the fact that the redhead simply wasn't Gerri. Gerri with her open face and her enthusiasm, her eagerness to learn something she wasn't good at. Gerri with her low self-image but keen sense of hu-mor, her generosity, the way she ate up life.

The redhead—whose name escaped him even though she'd told him twice—came in such a distant second to Gerri, it wasn't even a contest. He hadn't mentioned his birthday, hadn't wanted to share it with her. Even so, he tried to talk himself into it, tried to get enthusiastic about spending his birthday evening with a willing woman who had a body from a lingerie catalog, who offered only pleasure, no complications, no demands, no fragile egos.

Or so she seemed. He wouldn't be around to find

out, because in the morning, they would say goodbye; it had been his pattern, and he suspected it was hers, too.

He watched as the redhead slowly, enticingly circled her generous mouth with the tip of her tongue, then whispered, "It's getting crowded in here—want to go back to my place?"

Here it was, the moment most men lived their lives for. And his body was willing, that much he knew. Gerri wasn't available, he told himself, so what the hell. Why not?

He put money down on the counter to pay for their drinks as they both stood, a small smile of anticipation on her face. Taking her elbow, he walked her through the noisy casino—with its slots clanging, music blaring and loud conversations—into the cool night air of Virginia Street. Once there, he sucked in a huge breath.

"Want to follow me home?" the redhead purred. "I'm parked just down the block."

He took in another breath, then exhaled. "You know what, June?" Just in time, he remembered her name. "It's nothing to do with you, but I'm going to pass."

That wiped the smile off her face. "You're what?"

"I'm sorry, I'm just not feeling well."

"Oh. Well," she said silkily, wrapping her arms around his neck, pressing her perfect body to his, "come on back to my place and I'll make you feel a lot better."

Gently he unwound her arms and lowered them to her sides. "Sorry."

She stiffened. "I don't get it." Now he saw the

hurt, the insecurity, the real woman beneath the veneer, and wished he hadn't.

She deserved the truth. "I'm kind of hung up on someone else. She's out with another guy tonight."

Understanding dawned, and she laughed ruefully. "Oh, I get it. But you know," she said throatily, as she ran her long fingernails up and down his shirt buttons, "sometimes it helps to forget…with someone else."

"Sometimes it does. But not tonight."

Frowning, she flicked one of his buttons, then moved her hand so it was perched on her hip. "Well, shoot. I can't fight that one, can I?"

"Sorry," he said again, meaning it, then took her elbow again. "Come. I'll walk you to your car."

"Are you kidding?" She glanced at her watch. "It's only nine o'clock. The night's still young. I have two days off and I'm not going to waste them."

As she headed back to the casino, he called after her. "Good hunting."

She turned, gave it one last shot. "Sure you don't want to change your mind?"

"Believe me, June, if I were going to, it would be with you."

Her smile was full of regret, then she shrugged and sashayed back inside.

Des remained, alone once more, in the middle of the sidewalk. Happy revelers passed by, laughing excitedly. He glanced at his watch. Nine o'clock. She'd be at this event now with Rance. Again, jealousy hit his gut, hard, then rose to his throat, choking him.

He couldn't picture it, dammit, really he couldn't. Gerri didn't fit in with that party crowd. She wouldn't know how to play the game of polite chitchat with no substance. Hell, she didn't know how to lie politely, how to flirt. He wondered if she even knew how to dance.

He put his hands over his eyes, rubbing them. "Damn you, Gerri," he muttered. "Why aren't you here with me?"

Gerri nodded politely to the man she was dancing with. They'd been introduced, and she knew his name began with a *J*. Jack? John? Somewhere in the *J* spectrum. She hadn't been required to say much because he apparently loved the sound of his own voice; he'd been gifting her with it since the dance had begun.

She was relieved, really, at his nonstop verbiage, because it gave her a long-awaited chance to digest the evening's events so far. And, heavens, it was all quite, *quite* different from last week's dance.

Back then she'd stood on the sidelines for most of the night, awkward and alone. Once, Rance had taken pity on her and asked her to dance, but after she'd stepped on his toes several times, he'd stopped asking. Another couple of men had invited her to the dance floor—although she couldn't imagine why—but she'd turned them down, pleading that her ankle still hurt—the truth—but mostly because she sensed that her pathetic hairdo was coming undone. Maybe if she froze like a statue she could maintain an appearance of, please God, at least some dignity. Even so, she'd wound up tripping on her gown, tearing it and leaving a trail of hairpins wherever she'd gone.

However, that was then, this was now. Tonight, she'd been dancing steadily since arriving, and although swaying in rhythm or hopping and bobbing and gyrating her hips to a loud, insistent beat wasn't her strong suit, she'd managed all right, just by re-membering to follow her partner's lead instead of concentrating on what her own feet were doing.

It was kind of a terrific insight, actually: If you were self-conscious by nature, all you had to do was focus on what the other guy was doing, or saying, or needing, and you soon forgot to think about yourself and your shortcomings.

She hadn't tripped on her gown, not once! And her hair had stayed up, thanks to mousse and Didi's killer hairspray. With one glaring exception, it had been a perfect evening so far. She'd come here tonight as the new Gerri created by "the wish" and, buoyed by a self-assurance she didn't really possess, she continued to be a kind of minor sensation, and had been from the beginning.

That was only, she was sure, because she was the new kid in a sea of faces that were way too familiar to everyone there. As she and Rance had joined the party—he still making a big fuss about how gorgeous she looked and why had she been hiding herself all these months, while she kept smiling enigmatically and telling him she'd been there all the time and now it was time to hush up before he made a fool of both of them—most of the people in the already crowded ballroom paused to check her out.

She'd held her head high and, thank heavens, seemed to pass inspection. Several women wore el-bow-length gloves like the ones she had on; they too probably had short, stubby nails. She was struck once again by the extremely daring dresses she saw on several of the women, both young and not-so-young. See-through, low cut, form fitting, not a thing left to the imagination. Her dress was modest in comparison, which was good, because her endowments were, frankly, modest and then some. Although the neckline of the dress was cut so that you really couldn't tell.

She'd been to the ladies' room once, to refresh her lipstick, and had overheard the same two women from last week talking about her. One had been admiring, the other a bit catty, but she'd known to take both their opinions in stride and not let them affect her.

Last time, the fact that she'd been the topic of gossip had sent her fleeing into the night...and straight into Des's arms. Would that be repeated tonight?

Over her partner's shoulder—Jim? Jake?—she glanced at her watch. Ten-thirty. Another half hour to go, if she was supposed to recreate last week's event. But, *was* she supposed to do that?

Follow your heart, Cassie had told her.

"Hmm," Gerri said aloud.

"I'm sorry," her partner said. Josh? Jock? "Am I talking too much?"

"Not at all," she assured him. "It's fascinating."

Satisfied with her social lie, he prattled on, which gave her time to reflect some more.

After she'd exited the ladies' room, Rance had been waiting to introduce her to his mother. Louise Hays Wallace was tall and sharp-featured, her stark-white hair beautifully coiffed. She wore a long, dark blue satin gown, with a matching wrap around her shoulders and diamonds in her earlobes.

When Gerri had met her last week, the woman had been civil but subtly disdainful, which had made

Gerri shrink inside even more. They'd had a few polite words of conversation, mostly on the older
woman's part, as Gerri's usual loquaciousness failed
her utterly and she'd answered with one or two words,
all of a single syllable.

Tonight, the two women got along beautifully.

"What a lovely young woman you are," Rance's
mother said with a warm smile as they shook hands.
"And you own that delightful little bookstore on
West Liberty, near the museum. The Written Word.
I go there often."

"Yes, I recognized you, but I didn't know your
name."

"I don't remember seeing you there," she said
with a thoughtful frown.

Because I didn't look like this, Gerri almost said.
And you probably wouldn't have noticed me at all,
she would have added. Instead she decided the com-
ment needed no response and demurely kept her
mouth shut.

"Well, my dear," the older woman went on, "you
are a breath of fresh air, considering my son's usual
taste in females." With one hand on her hip, she
turned to Rance who had been standing by, unchar-
acteristically silent. "Why haven't I met Gerri before,
Rance?"

He shrugged. "I guess because this is our first
date."

Gerri added, "But we've known each other a
while, Mrs. Wallace."

"Louise, please."

"Louise," Gerri said warmly. She really did like
Rance's mother, with her sharp wit and forthright

manner, just as she'd suspected she would. "Rance is one of my regular customers."

Louise's eyebrows raised as she studied her son with skepticism. "You read? How interesting." To Gerri, she said, "Amazing how you can raise a child and not know him at all."

"Yes, I read," Rance replied, bristling. "I also think."

Gerri grabbed his elbow. "You promised you'd feed me an hour ago and I'm starving." She smiled at Louise. "We're going to the buffet. Can we get you anything?"

"No, thank you."

"I hope we'll get a chance to talk some more."

"Oh, we will," the older woman said with a knowing smile. "Count on it."

Now, as her dance partner continued his dissertation on annuities and tax loopholes, Gerri reflected on how amazing the encounter had been. So easy, so natural. Instead of thinking about how ugly she must look, how out of place, tonight's Gerri had concentrated on Rance and his mother, had been able to sense their natural antagonism, and done the diplomatic, friendly thing by rescuing him.

After all, she was here tonight because Rance had asked her a favor and she'd agreed. As a bonus, she'd made a favorable impression on his mother.

Not that she cared, really. Louise Wallace was nice under that haughty exterior, and it was always good to meet nice people. But there was still that one huge thing that was wrong with the evening. She was here, with Rance, but in body only.

Her mind—and her heart—were elsewhere.

With Des.

Follow your heart.

Rance tapped her partner on the shoulder. "Cutting in, Jeb."

Jeb. There we go. "Thanks so much, Jeb," she called out to him as she was whisked out of his arms and into a waltz.

"I can't take my eyes off you," Rance told her, gazing into her eyes with that impish grin on his face.

She found herself coloring slightly, which meant she might have been granted some grace and style for the night, but her skin still reacted the same. All that incredible charm of Rance's was now focused on her like a laser beam, and even her ninety-year-old grandma in the nursing home in upstate New York would have been affected. The man had charisma, no doubt about it.

"Stop," she said playfully. "You'll give me a swelled head."

Pulling her close, he whispered in her ear, "Do you mind if I tell you that looking at you is causing swelling in a different part of my anatomy?"

She knew she must be beet-red now. Other, more sophisticated women would hit that suggestive conversational gambit back over the net with ease, but not Gerri. "Yes," she said truthfully, "I do mind."

He pulled back to face her with a naughty little boy smile. "Not into the direct approach, huh? You prefer to take it slow, have me woo you first?"

"Not really," she said.

It wasn't so much the sexual innuendo in his remark, she realized, but that it had been made by the wrong man. With Des, she would have reacted with some abashment, too, because of her inexperience. But the truth was, it also probably would have turned her on, stoked an already simmering fire. Coming from Rance, it simply felt coarse, like a proposition in a bar.

Not his fault, that she knew. She'd been mooning over him for months, and he couldn't have missed it. He must have thought she'd jump at the chance to share his bed.

She punched his arm lightly. "Hey, you never did take me to the buffet table. I really need something in my stomach, to counteract the champagne."

"Why waste the champagne?"

Still waltzing, he steered her off the dance floor, away from the ballroom and onto the terrace. There, he backed her up against the railing, framed her face in his hands. "Gerri, Gerri, Gerri," he whispered, "my own little Cinderella."

Then he lowered his mouth to hers and kissed her.

Chapter Eight

He was a very practiced kisser, Gerri couldn't fail to notice, a man who really knew what he was doing. He began at a leisurely pace, his mouth moving over hers slowly, as though perusing the terrain before coming in for a landing. After a few moments, his tongue made flickering movements at the seam of her lips, eventually finding its way into her mouth with mounting aggression.

She stood there, letting him, wanting to—finally!—experience this kiss from the man who'd filled her daydreams for so long. But she really wasn't there. It felt as though the moment were happening to someone else. She felt…removed. While she could admire his technique, she simply couldn't get into the spirit of the thing.

Eventually Rance noticed her nonresponse and raised his head to stare at her. In the moonlight, his green-eyed gaze was puzzled. "Gerri?"

"Sorry. I'm just not—" Instead of finishing the sentence, she shrugged.

"Are you sick or something?"

Dear Rance. So sure of himself and his charisma, only an illness would keep a woman from eagerly returning his kisses. But, despite others' negative opinions of him, she genuinely liked the man, in a nonsexual way—although he wouldn't appreciate that fact—so she decided to let him down gently.

"Yes. I have a headache, I'm afraid." Another easily voiced social lie. "It's been coming on for a while. I think I'd better leave."

He frowned, still mystified by her behavior. "What are you talking about? What headache?"

Smiling, she put her fingers over his mouth. "You stay, okay? I'll take a taxi."

"But I—"

"Really, I'd prefer it. I had a lovely time, Rance. Thanks so much for asking me."

She felt his perplexed gaze on her back as she reentered the ballroom. Walking slowly, head held high, she took the first turn to the right to the bank of elevators.

When she was finally outside and at the top of the granite staircase that led to the street, she realized that more than anything, she wanted, *needed* to get away, not only from Rance, but from the whole world inside there in which she didn't belong and didn't want to belong. She wanted to hurry home to her cats and her little house and the safety and comfort there.

Feeling a rising urgency that she didn't understand, Gerri ran down the steps, looking down at her feet as she did, concentrating on not tripping. Last week that had been exactly what she'd done, stumbled and nearly taken a header, only just regaining her balance before it actually happened.

Once she landed safely on the sidewalk, she continued to run, rounding the corner at a swift pace.

"Oof!"

She crashed into a strong, solid chest with a force that should have knocked him cold, but the chest's owner remained upright. She was the one who felt on the verge of falling down, but strong hands gripped her upper arms and held her steady. Even before she looked up to see who it was, she knew.

Des.

She'd bumped smack into Des, just as she had last week. But this time, his face was a picture of fury; he seemed on the verge of attacking an arch enemy. Gasping, she stepped back from him and struggled to break his hold on her arms.

But he was having none of it. If anything, his grip tightened.

"Des!" she cried out, her heart thumping wildly. "You're hurting me!"

He didn't release her. Instead he shook her, hard. "I'm hurting you? Do you know how much you've hurt me?"

"What did I do? I don't understand."

"You don't, huh?" He shook her again.

"Please," she begged, thoroughly confused, "please, let me go."

"Gladly. After I do this."

He pulled her to him and, with a low growl, kissed—no, *devoured* her. As he thrust his tongue into her mouth, he released his grip on her arms. One hand went to the back of her head to hold her in place, while the other arm wrapped around her waist and pulled her as close as two bodies could be without fusing with each other.

His insistent tongue and lips forced her mouth to grant him access. His fingers were buried in her up-swept hairdo and she could just picture it coming apart. He tasted of alcohol, his grip on her made her feel like a prisoner, his anger terrified her. She tried to fight him off, but her strength was no match for his.

In one part of Des' brain, he sensed he was out of control. He'd been pacing the streets for what seemed like hours, trying to stifle the angry resentment that had been threatening to overtake him all evening. At the sight of Gerri, something snapped inside him. He wanted to punish her for hurting him, wanted to control her, wanted to imprint the taste of him on her flesh so she'd never forget him.

The other, civilized part of his brain registered her muffled protest, felt her hands trying to push him away. He knew suddenly that he'd crossed a line, one he'd never crossed before in his entire life.

He was trying to force himself on her. What kind of man did that?

Out of nowhere, a feeling welled up inside him that was far more overpowering than the rage. Oh God, he was hurting Gerri, causing pain to the woman he loved! Like that, the anger dissipated. In its place was soul-deep shame. Mortified, he relaxed the grip on her head, eased up on the pressure of his mouth on hers.

But, still, he couldn't let her go, was unwilling to stop kissing her, to break that precious contact. Placing the palms of his hands on her cheeks, and with all the tenderness in his heart, he showed her what he couldn't say aloud. Gently he kissed her eyes, her nose and, again, her mouth.

He fully expected her to push him away, and then to either flee or slap him—he deserved both. But, almost more amazing than this new feeling welling inside him, was the way Gerri responded. He felt her body's tension ease up as slowly, hesitantly, she stopped trying to push him away and, instead, wound her arms around his waist, then hugged him tightly.

She did break the kiss for a brief moment. Gazing up at him with eyes shining through tears, she said, "Oh, Des, Des," then joined her mouth to his with as much eagerness as she'd tried to fight him off just seconds before.

It was a Friday night in Reno. The sidewalks were full, with all kinds of people going by. Des and Gerri were locking lips in full view of every one of them, but he didn't care. He was transported into another dimension, a world where the two of them had no past hurts, no missed messages, no barriers between them.

Only love could accomplish this. Yes, love.

He loved her.

He felt it fill him, felt the joy of the realization almost bursting out of him. "Gerri," he murmured, then angled her head for a deeper, more emotional kiss.

She answered his need, her tongue meeting his eagerly, each of them trying to be part of the other. She couldn't have missed his growing arousal, straining insistently against her stomach, just as he felt the hardened points of her breasts pressing against his shirt. Groaning, he ran his hands over her bare shoulders and arms, but enough awareness of their surroundings kept him from doing what he really wanted to do, which was to fondle her breasts, to reach between her thighs and caress the warm, moist womanly essence of her.

Oh, how he wanted to take her somewhere, right this moment, and pour all his love into her.

Oh, how he wanted—

"Hey! Quinlan! Let her go!"

The voice came from behind him as he felt someone tap him hard on his shoulder. Startled, both he and Gerri broke off the kiss but kept their arms wrapped around each other.

He angled his head to see Rance, all dressed up in a tux, his fists clenched at his sides, a look of fury on his face that might have matched Des's insides just moments ago.

The other man pushed at Des's shoulder. "Break it up, okay? Take your hands off her."

Gerri felt as though she'd just been harshly awakened from a dream. Images flashed through her mind, one after the other, at breakneck speed. Angry Des, assaulting and terrifying her. Gentle and loving Des, erasing the previous ugly image. And now, here came irate Rance, spoiling for a fight.

The dream was fast becoming a nightmare.

Des, however, seemed to have collected himself, and refused to take the other man up on his challenge. Letting go of Gerri, he held up both hands in a pacifying gesture. "Hey, don't, okay? Everything's fine."

But clearly, Rance wasn't in a diplomatic mood. He shoved Des's shoulder again, harder this time. "Yeah? I don't think so. I don't think making a spectacle of yourself in the middle of the sidewalk is fine. Not with *my* date."

A few passersby stopped to check out the cause of the loud voices they were hearing. Gerri glanced at them, then at Des and Rance. She placed a trembling hand on the latter's arm. "Rance? It's okay, really it is."

Shaking off her hand, he glared at her. "Oh, is it? I kiss you and you have a headache? He kisses you and the headache's gone?"

"You kissed her?" Des said, and like that, the hostile Des was back.

"Hell, yes, I kissed her. And she seemed to like it a lot."

"Did she?" Des's voice was quiet now, but menacing, as he pushed Rance's shoulder back aggressively.

As more onlookers gathered, excited murmurs passed information to the newcomers to the scene.

"Damn straight," Rance said. "What a surprise, huh? Our little bookworm has been hiding her real self for quite a while, and let me tell you, she's hot."

With a growl, Des started toward Rance again. Gerri cried out, "Des, stop it. Please."

"Why? So he can insult you again?" He spiked her with a look that said she ought to be pleased he was defending her honor.

Then, for the first time, Des seemed to take in her appearance. The gown, the hair—which, miraculously, was still in place—the gloves, the makeup. A look of astonishment came over his face as he raked her up and down with his gaze.

"Des?" she said, taken aback. "What is it?"

"You— You're—" He seemed unable to finish his sentence.

"I'm what?" Uncertain, her hand flew to her chest.

He gestured at her outfit. "Beautiful." But it didn't come out admiringly. It was more like he wasn't sure just how he felt about it.

"Yes, she is," Rance crowed. "And she's with me tonight, so back off."

Des continued to stare at her. "Is that what you want me to do, Gerri? Back off?"

"No, but—" she began.

"Better believe it," Rance snarled.

"You shut up," Des snapped, searing him with another hostile look, "or I'll make you wish you had."

Someone in the crowd who'd gathered around them now mentioned the police. Someone else told them not to spoil the fun.

Gerri was getting irritated. "What's the matter with me looking beautiful for one night?" she asked, hands on hips and still back on the previous exchange between Des and her. "Aren't I allowed?"

Des turned back to her, obviously fighting for control of his temper as he spoke to her. "Nothing's wrong with it," he said. "It's just that, well, I guess I'm not used to you, well—" he nodded to her gown "—like this. You don't look like…you."

"Well, tough. I'm still me, whatever I look like!"

Apparently Rance didn't relish being thrust aside and told to shut up. He grabbed Des's shoulders and turned him around, away from Gerri. "Hey, I'm not finished with you yet."

"Stop it, Rance." Gerri implored, gripping his arm and trying to pull him away, but he ignored her.

"Why don't you take a hike?" He sneered at Des.

"Why don't you get screwed?" Des sneered back, and suddenly the two of them were struggling with each other, each trying to land a punch, with neither of them connecting.

Jostling Gerri to the side, the crowd made a circle around them, their faces excited and animated at the prospect of a fight. Again, someone mentioned the police. Gerri pulled at her hair with her fingers. If the hairspray hadn't been so effective, she might have yanked some of it out.

She tried one last time. "Cut it out, both of you! You're behaving like adolescents!" she screamed, but neither of them seemed to hear her.

Disgusted with the whole situation, she threw her hands up in the air, then pushed her way through the crowd. "Men. Idiots, all of them," she muttered as she headed down the street to find a taxi.

The dress was back in its garment bag, not a stain or a tear anywhere on it, as pristine as it had been before she put it on, thankfully. The borrowed jewelry was wrapped in plastic for safekeeping. She'd removed all the combs, hairpins and pearls from her hair and given it a good brushing. She'd washed her face, bathed, and donned a nightgown and robe. Nightly rituals completed.

However, although it was nearly one o'clock in the morning, Gerri realized she still wasn't ready to sleep, so she decided to go downstairs to make herself a cup of hot chocolate. Soon she was nestled in her favorite corner of the couch, Ashley stretched out across her lap and George managing to curl himself up on part of her upper chest and left shoulder, his rumbling purr loud enough to set off an earthquake warning system.

Gerri sipped the hot, sweet, soothing drink, then rested her tired head against the back couch cushion. Finally she could replay and analyze the evening she'd just been through.

"Good Lord," she said with a loud sigh. What a mess it had turned into. She'd done the fund-raiser "right," then wound up between two men, both of them fighting over her. Practically pistols at dawn. There were those, she imagined, who would find that kind of thing fascinating, even flattering. Not Gerri. Personally, she was totally turned off.

She was also bewildered.

Rance, she was pretty sure she could figure out. In kissing her on the terrace, he was letting her know that he had decided to single her out from the crowd for his attention, an action which would have pleased most women. However, his pride must have been affected by her disinterest in getting physical with him, so by the time he'd come upon her giving Des what he'd been denied, his bruised ego had twisted the scene around so that he could be her rescuer, a role many men found suited them well.

When it became obvious she didn't need rescuing, again that inflated ego of his reacted by accusing her of being some kind of femme fatale who'd purposely hidden her allure behind bookishness. After that, both he and Des baited each other until it was impossible, given the testosterone-driven competitive nature of the male animal, not to get violent.

But Des—what to make of him? Angry with her, then tender toward her, then protective of her—that guy thing, again. From there, stunned by her appearance and not sure he liked her to look that way. And back one more time to anger, but this time at Rance.

The man had been all over the map, mood-wise.

Yet, underneath it all, she'd sensed his torment. He was as bewildered by his own behavior as she was. And, darn it, it got to her, so she couldn't sit here right now and resent him as much as he deserved.

"Don't you dare," she said out loud. But even as she counseled herself not to get all teary-eyed about Des's inner turmoil—he'd put her through the ringer that evening, for heaven's sake!—she still found her eyes filling up.

She reached for the box of tissues on the side table. Instead her fingers touched another object.

The magic glasses.

She picked them up and studied them. Still rhinestone-studded, still absurd-looking. But they had powers, for sure. She could bear witness to that.

If she could make another wish, what would it be? To get some insight into Des, maybe to decipher what his real feelings for her were? To know her own feelings about him? To get a normal person's brain instead of a nerdy scholar's?

But no. There was a caveat that came with the glasses: one wish only, Cassie had said. Well, Gerri had made that wish. Gerri had gotten that wish. And now Gerri was stuck with its consequences.

Nothing, but nothing had turned out the way she'd

hoped it would. Sure, she'd looked lovely at the ball, but that was cosmetic—same package, different wrapping. Sure, she'd finally gotten Rance's interest, but he wasn't the one whose interest she'd wanted. And she'd only snagged that interest because of her gussied-up appearance.

Lesson: It was just as bad being valued for one's outsides only as being rejected for one's brains.

The ringing of the doorbell startled her out of her contemplative state. Des! He'd come to apologize, or to explain, or whatever. Her heart leaped at the thought of him out there, in the night, standing on her doorstep. They would talk this thing through, make a real attempt to understand each other.

Quickly she rose and, patting down her hair so it wouldn't appear flyaway, she went to the door and peered through the peephole.

Not Des, she observed with a sinking heart. The other one. Rance. She was treated to his face, up close and smiling crookedly at her. His teeth were very white, his hair was mussed, his satin bow tie was missing, and his right eye was swollen shut.

Gerri opened the door, but kept the screen door latched. Folding her arms over her chest, she said frostily, "What do you want?"

His smile was sheepish. "You were…on my way home."

"Fine. Go there."

"But, I need to explain." His words were slurred, and he wiped around his mouth with his fingers as though that would fix it. Was he drunk? she wondered.

"See, I thought you were…mine," he explained.

"Tonight, I mean. But I shouldn't have said all that stuff back there," he went on. Then a look of surprise crossed his face as his leg gave out from under him. He managed to keep from falling by clutching the side of the door.

Slurred words. Loss of balance. Uh-oh, Gerri realized. During the fight, Rance might have gotten a concussion.

Quickly she unlocked the screen door. "Come in."

He stumbled across the threshold, but she grabbed him before he fell. There was no smell of alcohol on his breath.

"You're hurt. Did you drive yourself here in this condition?" she asked him, struggling to hold him upright.

When he nodded, she shook her head. "I hope you didn't kill anybody."

"Not a one," he said, "but I have a bitch of a headache. And I need to sit down."

Gerri led him over to the couch and he collapsed onto it. Then he gazed up at her through pain-filled eyes, even as his mouth made an attempt to smile again. "Did I apologize?"

"Yes."

"I'm sorry."

"So you said," she responded dryly. "I think we'd better get you to the hospital."

"Not necessary," he said, surprising her by yanking her arms so that she plopped down onto the sofa beside him. Awkwardly he leaned over to kiss her, but she turned her head away so that his mouth landed on her ear. She scrambled to get up again, and he fell sideways; now his upper body lay sprawled across the cushions, his legs still on the floor.

"Guess you don't want to kiss me," Rance mumbled and with that, closed his eyes and passed out.

Worried, Gerri gazed down on him. She tried to remember what she'd read about concussions. Was it better to let them sleep or to keep them awake by walking them? Or was that what you did after an overdose of sleeping pills? Whatever, it wouldn't do to take any chances.

She called the emergency room of the hospital and they told her, if she could manage, to bring him in. After quickly throwing on some clothes, she managed, but not easily. She half pulled and half supported Rance into her Toyota, then maneuvered her way around his little sports car, and drove him to the hospital.

The doctor on duty told her the concussion seemed light, but he'd be keeping Rance overnight to run some tests. The nurse assured her they would contact his family, and so Gerri left, driving again through the star-filled night, up the narrow road to her house.

By the time she got there, it was nearly four in the morning, and, finally, she was exhausted enough to sleep. What should she make of all this? she wondered as she parked again in her spot next to the garage. Two men in one night, determined to not just kiss her, but to *own* her. One of them, in fact, had made a second attempt despite a concussion. The wrong one offered apologies that she wanted to hear from the other.

Should she be flattered by all this attention? Because all she felt was distaste. Little boys, both of

them, with their oversized egos. Egos that had caused
one of them to wind up in the hospital.

How had Des fared in the fight? she wondered,
nibbling her bottom lip worriedly as she made her
way into her house. Better than Rance? Or, God for-
bid, a lot worse? Once inside she called the hospital
again, this time to see if Des had wound up there. But
he hadn't. Which was good news. Maybe.

She tried to swat away the concern she felt, telling
herself that Des was a strong, sturdy man, probably
in better shape than Rance, and he would have han-
dled himself just fine. Go to bed, she instructed herself. He's a grown-up—even if he didn't act like one
earlier. He was responsible for himself.

Still, even after she'd turned out all the lights and
climbed the stairs to her bedroom, locking the door
behind her just in case; even after she'd crawled into
bed for the night, both cats in place, she couldn't
silence the small voice of fear for Des.

As she closed her eyes, she prayed for his safety.

Even if she never wanted to see the jerk again.

SATURDAY: The sky was that misty pale gray it
took on just before dawn. The road was empty and
quiet, except for the sound of his truck's gears as it
made its way up to Gerri's place. Outside his window,
a couple of birds hooted at each other; in the distance,
a cock crowed.

Another day had passed. Des was officially thirty-
five, but this morning he was tired enough, and must
look it, to pass for ten years older.

What a jerk he'd been last night. A bloody, stupid

jerk. He hadn't acted this badly since... Hell, he couldn't remember ever behaving this badly.

Maybe when he was an eight-year-old and he came home from school to find his mother was gone and wasn't coming back. He'd cried then, and kicked things, had acted out by cutting school and getting into trouble. But it was insignificant trouble, a few minor fights, swiping gum at the candy store and getting caught, refusing to speak for days. Kid-in-pain stuff.

The way he'd conducted himself yesterday, well, there had been no excuse for it, and he was here to tell Gerri just that. He rubbed his hand over his jaw and then flexed it. Rance had landed a good one there. Man, that hurt, he thought, wincing with pain. But it had been worth it; he'd gotten in a good one to Rance's eye before a couple of guys in the crowd had broken up the fight. Afterward, he and Rance had been encouraged to shake hands, but neither of them was willing, so they'd both gone their separate ways, Des back to his ranch and Rance, to who knew where, and who cared?

Des had showered and napped a couple of hours, before he'd awoken with a start and knew what he had to do. He would make it all right with Gerri, on his knees if necessary. This blossoming love for her had thrown him for a loop, had made him act like a crazy man. He would take her recriminations without flinching because he deserved them. And because she was worth it.

During his one moment of sanity last evening—when she'd returned his kiss with gusto, even after he'd been so rough on her—he'd known then.

She cared about him. Just as he cared about her.

There was something special between them, a bond that was friendship and sex and feelings that were deeper and longer lasting than either of those two.

Love.

A simple word, but one that said it all.

He glanced at his watch. It was still pretty early. He might wake her up, but she'd get past that when she heard what he had to say. Besides, she was usually out riding her horse around this time of morning, so she must be an early riser.

He maneuvered his truck around the last bend, the one that led to her driveway. As her house came into view, he slammed his foot on the brake. Then he sat, stone-still, and stared.

Behind Gerri's car, there was another, parked at a crooked angle. It was a convertible, its top down, a little Italian sports job.

Like that, the miserable, sick feeling was back, the bile rising in the back of his throat. He tried to control it, tried not to jump to conclusions. But he had a sneaking suspicion he knew who the car belonged to. Keeping his truck where it was, back from the house, he turned off the engine and got out. As quietly as he could, he walked over the gravel and up to the sports car. He peered at the license plate. It was a vanity one: RANCE III it read.

He glanced at the house—all was in darkness. Not a light on anywhere.

God, how he'd searched for a reasonable explanation for what was staring him in the face, but he couldn't come up with one. Except the obvious.

Gerri and Rance were in there. Together. More than likely in her bed.

It hurt. Oh man, it hurt. He was past jealousy, over his rage. What remained was a deep, terminal laceration way down in the center of his soul. He stood there in Gerri's driveway for quite a while, his arms folded over his gut, his eyes squeezed shut with misery. So then, he told himself, that was the way it was. He'd made a fool of himself the night before, and for no reason at all. She'd made her choice, and she hadn't picked him.

Slowly he walked back to his truck, his shoulders slumped, his jaw aching more than ever. He pulled out of her driveway and began the journey back to his ranch.

Happy birthday, he told himself quietly. Maybe now he would learn, really take in the lesson that had been staring him in the face his entire life.

When you opened up your heart, you got kicked in the face for caring too much.

For a short while, he'd thought Gerri would be different, that she would be the one who wouldn't let him down.

But, just like every important woman in his life before her, she'd decided he was dispensable.

Chapter Nine

"He did *what?*"

This was not the first time Didi had responded this way to Gerri's recounting of last night's events. They were in a cozy corner of Didi's shop, each in an antique armchair, sipping the freshly brewed coffee that Didi kept on hand for her customers.

Gerri had just told her the part about Rance's late-night knock on the door. "Yes, he just showed up, with a black eye and a concussion. And he tried to kiss me again. And then he passed out."

"You're kidding."

"So I took him to the hospital and they said he'd be okay. He is. I called this morning. Not that I care. Except I do, kind of. You know."

Didi, who had been leaning forward in amazement during Gerri's entire recitation, finally sat back in her chair, shook her head and said, "Wow."

Gerri nodded. "Yes. Wow, indeed."

"Now that's what I call a full evening."

"Too full."

Didi whistled in amazement. "Two of them, both of them behaving like complete morons."

"True."

Taking another sip of her coffee, Didi contemplated all the information she'd just been given. Then she met Gerri's gaze again. "So, how do you feel today?"

"About which part?"

"I don't know—everything. Still got the hots for Rance?"

"Hah! Not in the least," Gerri said emphatically.

"Well that's good, anyway. And you got to go to the fund-raiser with him, and knocked everyone's socks off, right? That had to feel terrific."

"It did. At first. But I don't know, after a while it didn't mean much."

Didi nodded philosophically. "Yeah. That old what's-left-when-your-dreams-come-true? thing."

"Kind of."

"So then...I guess we're left with what's-his-name."

She made a face of self-disgust. "Des."

"Des, the dark horse." Didi probed her friend's facial expression thoroughly, then pronounced, "You're getting hung up on the guy, aren't you?"

Gerri averted her gaze; she felt vaguely ashamed. "I know I shouldn't but, well, I'm worried about him."

"Because...?"

"Well, I mean, Rance had a concussion. What about Des? What if Rance hurt him, badly? What if he's lying in an alley somewhere, wounded and alone?''

"Aren't we being just a bit melodramatic?"

"Maybe. But—'' She left the sentence unfinished, and scratched her head. Her hair was back in its pony-tail, but her scalp was still a bit tender. One more lesson: Complicated, elegant hairdos didn't just happen without paying a price.

"But what? Out with it," Didi demanded.

"I want to call him," she blurted out, "find out if he made it home okay, find out how he is."

Her friend stared at her then shook her head sadly. "If I told you not to, would it keep you from doing it?"

"Why shouldn't I?"

"Well, for one, it would be the least cool thing you could do."

"It would?"

Didi nodded. "Oh *amiga,* no self-respecting woman would call up a man who treated her this badly. This guy is obviously trouble, more than you can cope with. But if there's any hope for the two of you, *he* has to be the one to call *you.* He has to tell you he's sorry and ask for your forgiveness. See, if you keep making it easy for him, he stops holding up his end of the relationship."

"We don't have a relationship."

"Sure you do. Keep this up and, trust me, he'll lose respect for you."

Gerri grimaced. "But what if he's hurt and he can't call?"

"Believe me, if it's bad, you'll hear about it soon enough."

"Oh."

Gerri made herself consider her friend's advice. After all, Didi was pretty wise in areas where Gerri was totally inadequate, one of the reasons their friendship worked so well.

Not for the first time, she wished she were a little more in the know when it came to relationships, she thought, taking a sip of her coffee. Or did she? Maybe she was all right not knowing. Maybe she needed to be true to herself, not to some proscribed code of behavior.

"I suppose all this don't-call-him-until-he-calls-you stuff comes under the heading of dating etiquette, huh."

"Yup."

"Well, I've never been much good at that kind of thing, so why would I start now?" With a deep, resigned sigh, Gerri rose from her chair. "Thanks for listening. You're a doll. I have to get back to the shop. Connie called in sick and I've left Melissa alone there."

Didi walked her to the door, nodding to a couple of customers as she did. When they got there, she put a hand on the doorknob and said, "You're going to call him, aren't you?"

Gerri looked down at her feet. "Thanks again for last night—the dress, the hair, all of it," she replied, instead of responding to Didi's question.

"Yeah, you are. You're going to call him." Didi's smile was rueful. "Hey, who am I to give advice?" she said, squeezing Gerri's shoulder. "I date a lot, but nothing lasts. I may know the rules, but I still sleep alone."

Grateful for her friend's understanding, Gerri hugged her, then tried to explain. "Oh, Didi. It's just that...I really care about him. There's something about Des, some broken part of him that calls to me. This will sound weird, but I have a broken part, too, and when I'm with him, it's like the two broken parts fit together and become whole...and not broken anymore." She shook her head. "I know I'm not making any sense."

Never before had she seen such a tender look of yearning on Didi's face. "Oh, yeah, *amiga*," she said softly, "you're making a lot of sense. Go get him." She opened the door and Gerri stepped out into the sun-filled day.

"And listen," Didi added as Gerri was about to leave.

"What?"

"I want details, okay?"

Even though she still wondered if she was a fool, the minute she got back to her shop, Gerri looked up Des's number. Then, heart pounding, she punched in the numbers.

He picked up on the third ring. "Hello?"

"Des?" she said brightly. "Hi, it's Gerri."

There was a beat before he said, "Oh, hi." He sounded completely disinterested, even cold.

She swallowed before she continued, "I just wondered how you are."

"I'm fine."

She waited, hoping he'd elaborate, but he didn't.

"I was worried about you," she admitted, squeezing her eyes tightly as though waiting for a blow. "I mean, did Rance hurt you or anything? He wasn't in great shape, so I wondered how you were.''

"I'm fine, I told you. Not a mark on me.'' She might have detected a hint of male pride there, but still his tone remained singularly uninviting. It was as though a chill was flowing through the wires, from his end to hers.

"Oh," she said, kicking herself for not listening to Didi. ''Well, okay then. That's all I wanted to know.''

She was about to hang up when he spoke again. "I'm glad you called.''

Her heart soared with relief, until she heard the next sentence. ''Look, I want to come down there and get my poems back.''

"You what?''

"My poems. I'm going to be in town later today and I thought I'd pick them up then.''

"But, I haven't had a chance to read them yet.''

"That's okay. I've decided that I don't want you to publish them. Or anyone, for that matter.''

"Oh.'' The sudden stab of grief she felt was so deep, she was unable to say anything else.

"I'll see you later.'' And with that, he hung up.

She stared at the receiver for a few moments, raw with a sense of betrayal she wasn't sure she'd ever experienced before, not even when she'd found out about Tommy's perfidy. It felt as though every part of her hurt. Blood, bones, pores. Brain, heart, spirit. She closed her eyes, unable to bear it.

But she didn't cry. She didn't wonder what she'd done wrong. She didn't call herself names. No, none of that old behavior. She didn't deserve this. Nothing she could have done warranted Des's icy attitude.

The anger began slowly. It started as a trickle of indignation, then grew to resentment, then grew and grew some more, until it became a full, no-holds-barred rage, completely laying to waste her pain.

"You creep!" she said out loud.

"What did you say?" Melissa called out from the biography section, where she was dusting the shelves. "Do you need me?"

"No, it was nothing," Gerri called back. "Nothing at all."

By the time Des walked into the shop in the late afternoon, Gerri had been nursing her anger for a long time. She glanced up as the bell went off, then returned her attention once more to the pile of receipts she'd been trying to sort, in between customers, for the past two hours. She felt him staring at her, but refused to acknowledge his presence.

It wasn't until he was at the counter, standing right in front of her, that she raised her head to meet his gaze. "Yes?" she said.

Des seemed taken aback by her less-than-civil greeting. "I'm here."

"So I see," she said coldly, amazed at how easily she could turn off her usual good nature this way. But the man well and truly deserved it.

"Do you have them? My poems?"

"Right here." She practically shoved the manila envelope at him, then went back to her receipts.

He shifted his feet awkwardly, seemed on the verge of saying something, then grunted, "Thanks," and headed for the exit.

"Wait just a minute!"

Every eye in the place turned toward the sound of a loud, angry woman's voice. Gerri, realizing that she'd drawn attention to herself, glanced around at her customers, then at Melissa's wide-eyed look of astonishment. It wouldn't do to make a scene, not here in her beloved bookstore.

Coming around the counter, she joined Des at the door.

"I'll be back in a few minutes," she told Melissa. Then to Des, she said, "I'll walk you out."

"No need."

"Oh, yes, there is."

When they were on the sidewalk, she said, "Take a walk with me, okay?"

"No need," he said again.

"Yes, there is," she repeated, even more emphatically, unwilling to brook any arguments.

She started off in the direction of the nearby park and was gratified to realize that he was following her. No way he was getting away with being surly, no way he was leaving her presence today without giving her some good solid answers to his behavior. And no way was he getting away today without taking with him a piece of her mind.

There was something freeing, cleansing, really, about this righteous rage. It was downright exhilarating! Sure, she'd been angry before, but her usual way to deal with it was to stuff it down and then blame herself. Well, not today, by God. Not today.

Wordlessly she led him to the fountain near the children's swings, stopped at the handrail that surrounded the water-spewing sculpture, gripped the top rail and stared at the spray of water as it gushed upward into the clear blue sky.

Des stood a few steps away from her, also at the railing. "What do you want?" he said warily.

She turned and stared right into those blue, blue eyes of his. "I want to know why you're punishing me."

Instead of answering, he turned his gaze to the fountain, the muscles in his jaw working for several beats before he answered. "I wasn't aware I was doing that."

"Well, let me make you aware of it then. Why?"

Again, he didn't respond right away, and she sensed his inner struggle to come up with the right reply.

"Don't think of what you want to say. Just say it!" Really, the man could try Buddha's patience.

His head jerked in her direction. "Okay. I don't like the fact that you canceled our dinner last night to go to this thing with Rance. It was my birthday."

"But you told me to go."

"You shouldn't have listened."

"You shouldn't have asked me to read your mind!" It wasn't like Gerri to snap back like this, but boy, did it feel great.

He opened his mouth to respond, then shut it again. Shrugging, he said nothing. But his expression remained stony.

She studied him, the fierce brow, the downward turn of his mouth. Portrait of a man in turmoil, she thought, and felt some of her own anger abating.

No! Hold on to it, she urged herself silently. He's not off the hook yet.

She leaned an elbow on the railing and angled her body so she could face him. "So that's it? You're upset with me because of your birthday?" When, once again, he raised and lowered his shoulders, she shot back, "Hey, don't shrug me off. Don't pull that silent male stuff on me here. I'm trying to understand. Help me."

Gerri's adamant words and attitude hit Des like a body blow, and he felt backed against a wall, which he absolutely detested. He wished he could just walk away. He hated arguments; but more than that, he hated having Gerri so pissed off at him. He'd hurt her, that was clear. But dammit, she'd hurt him, too.

"Okay. I don't like the fact that you went to the damn thing with Rance," he said, and before he could stop himself, added, "and even more than that, that you kissed him."

"So I kissed him. I kissed you, too, and I didn't ask his permission."

"Did you kiss him with the same enthusiasm you showed me?" he barked.

For a brief moment, she seemed confused. Then, as realization dawned, her eyes widened. "Des. You're jealous."

The look of surprised wonder on her face made him cringe. Even so, he wasn't able to stop himself from saying, "Damn right I am!"

She seemed to give herself a moment to savor his jealousy, but then it was gone. Shaking her head like his explanation wasn't acceptable, she placed her hands on her hips and glared at him, really getting worked up now. "Was that what was going on with you when I ran into you? Why were you so angry?

Why did you attack me that way? You scared me to death.''

Muttering a curse, he closed his eyes and shook his head. "I know," he growled. "I feel bad about that."

"Hallelujah," Gerri said, throwing a hand up in the air. "The man finally admits he played some part in this."

"Yes, okay?" he flared back at her. "I'm admitting it. I was out of line. Satisfied?"

With his apology, lame as it was, some of the heat seemed to go out of her. "Well, good then," Gerri said, less assertive now. "It's just that..." Her belligerent expression changed, softened. "Oh, Des, I don't understand why you were *so* angry at me. I mean, it seemed way over the top. Will you at least tell me why?"

Please don't go there, he thought, closing his eyes against her sweet, confused face. "It won't happen again."

"Oh, good," she said derisively. "Another non-answer."

Her sarcasm made him open his eyes again to see her whirl around and then stomp away from him. She made it halfway around the fountain, then turned around and came back, obviously frustrated with him, but unable to just walk away. That made two of them, he thought.

Folding her arms across her chest, she glared at him, her mouth in a thin line. That went on for a while before she sighed and placed a tentative hand on his arm. He felt her gentling, becoming more of the old Gerri, the one he liked so very much.

She even looked like the old Gerri today, none of

that…elegance of last night, her hair back in its usual ponytail, another long, shapeless jumper on her slender body, loafers on her feet.

"Des? At least tell me why you've asked for your poems back."

Damn. Question after question after question. And he wished she hadn't asked that one. But he knew she deserved an answer. "They're…personal," he mumbled.

"All poetry is personal."

"Maybe they're too personal to have anyone else read them."

"But you *did* give them to me to read." Her hazel eyes invited him to confide in her. "That had to mean something."

"Yeah, well."

He pushed away from the railing and walked over to a nearby bench and sat down. God, how he wished she would stop probing and pushing the way she did. He didn't do well being interrogated. Gerri followed him, sat next to him. He felt small, and vaguely childish, and he hated it.

"Maybe I trusted you with them," he said, trying to be as truthful as he could, "and I don't trust easily."

"I think I knew that," she answered quietly. "And I was honored."

She wanted more, of course. But he didn't know what to say now. When he wrote his poetry, the words flowed onto the page. But he lacked that ability when confronted with a live person.

Go away, Gerri, he wanted to say. *Don't waste your questions on me.*

But, true to form, she was still in there hacking away at the problem—which was him—and trying to formulate a theory. "You're saying you trusted me then. Why don't you trust me now?" There was so much bewilderment, so much hurt in her expression, he wished he could just disappear so he wouldn't have to see it.

Okay, she wanted to know, he would tell her. "I came to your house this morning," he said gruffly. "I intended to apologize for my behavior last night."

Her eyebrows shot up in surprise. "You did? I didn't see you."

"I didn't come to the door."

"For heaven's sake, why not?"

"I figured you didn't want to be disturbed," he said pointedly.

She didn't seem to get it. Instead she smiled at him, for the first time since they'd begun this conversation. Not her open, sunny Gerri smile. Instead it was one of her self-effacing grins. "Yeah, I was kind of tired. When I finally conked out last night I slept like a log. I almost missed opening time at the shop."

Now her expression became chiding. "But, Des, you could have rung the bell, could have woken me up, it would have been okay."

"With you, maybe. But not with Rance."

There, he thought. He couldn't have said it any plainer.

"Rance?" At first she seemed puzzled, but then the dawning light of realization made her eyes open wide with dismay. "You thought I was with Rance? I mean, like in the biblical sense?"

"I sure did. I figured he was in your bed. His car

was there, the lights were out. Do the numbers.'' He stared down at his hands, wanting this conversation to be over.

"But…God, you're so wrong. Rance spent the night in the hospital. You gave him a concussion, for heaven's sake,'' she said.

The look he slanted her was one of pure skepticism. "A concussion? I barely hit the guy. And if he was at the hospital, how did his car get to be at your place?''

"He stopped off on his way home and passed out. I had to take him to the hospital. Hey, if you don't believe me, call them. Call him.'' Obviously annoyed with him, she stabbed his chest with her index finger. "You're totally off-base here, admit it.''

"Can you blame me?'' he shot back. "I mean, you've had a crush on the guy for a while.''

Her eyes widened with horror. "How did you know that?''

"Your voice changed whenever you talked about him,'' he said with disgust. "And you got this goofy expression…''

"Really? I was that transparent?''

When he nodded, she clutched her hands together and gazed off into the distance. "I hate that about myself. My face registers everything. Absolutely no subtlety whatsoever.''

"It's one of the things I like about you,'' he found himself saying. "You don't play games.''

"I don't know how. Didi says I'm hopeless.''

"Don't learn. I hate games.''

Like that, as though all the air had been let out of a balloon, their heated exchange was over. They sat in silence, each involved in their own thoughts, for a little while.

Des just about hated himself. Jumping to conclusions, ready to believe the worst of Gerri, because he believed the worst of people, in general. He felt so tired, worn out from all the emotion. He wanted to be alone, but he couldn't make himself get up.

A small rubber ball bounced at his feet. He picked it up just as a toddler came running up to him. Smiling despite himself, he tossed the ball to the little boy who grinned, revealing three tiny upper teeth and two lower ones, then ran off.

Gerri was the one who broke the silence. "I guess you really were jealous, huh. I'm not used to arousing that emotion in men."

Damn right I was jealous, he wanted to say. Eaten up with it. Sick with it. Out of my mind, in fact. But he couldn't cop to it. It seemed so…weak. So he shrugged.

Wordlessly they gazed at each other. She hadn't slept with Rance, but that didn't make everything magically all better. There were so many questions of his own he wanted to ask her. What do I mean to you? How do you feel about Rance now? Do you still have a crush on him?

Choose me, he wanted to say.

Pathetic, absolutely pathetic.

"Des?"

"What?"

Gerri knew if she didn't say it now, she'd never get a chance again. According to Didi's definition, it would make her the furthest thing from cool as it was possible to be. But she wasn't cool, not in the least.

And most definitely not when it came to matters of the heart.

"I don't understand you," she admitted. "I mean, I think I understand parts of you, but then you throw me a curve and I realize I don't know what to say or how to act. And—" She drew in a deep breath. "It matters because, well, I...have feelings for you. Lots of them."

He glanced at her quickly, hope flaring briefly in his blue-eyed gaze. For a moment, he seemed on the verge of saying something. But the moment passed and he looked away and nodded. Back to preverbal body language, were they? Did that mean he had feelings for her, too? The good news. Or that he knew she had them for him? Not so good.

Did being jealous signal having romantic feelings or just possessiveness? Should she just burst out with it? *I love you, you jerk,* she contemplated telling him. *Despite all the ups and downs and yin and yangs and pushes and pulls between us, I love you.*

And, by the way, you need to do some serious work on your head.

In agony, she waited for Des to say something, anything. He raked his upper lip with his teeth, then shook his head, slowly, sadly. "I have feelings for you too, Gerri. But," he added quietly, "I'm... scarred. I don't think I ever knew how much before. I make assumptions that aren't right. I don't trust easily and I don't get over betrayal at all."

"So," she said haltingly, "somehow, I abused your trust. I betrayed you."

"When you explain it, of course you didn't."

"I felt betrayed, too, you know."

"I don't blame you."

"So, then where does that leave us?" *Please, Des,* she willed him. *Let me in.*

"You have…a different nature than I do," he began haltingly, then sighed and shook his head. "I wish I could be more like you, but I don't know how not to be this way. People don't change. I guess no one gets over their mother walking out on them, and I'm no different from anyone else. And I'm beginning to see that I need to take at least half the responsibility for Stella's leaving. Sure, she wanted more than ranch life, but I was always waiting for her to walk out anyway, so it wasn't a stretch for her to just get up and go." Angling his head, he met her gaze. His eyes seemed older than his years, weighted down with old pain. "What I'm saying is that I don't think I'm a good prospect…for you, or for anyone."

With that, he seemed to be done. He'd said a lot, used more words in one stretch than she'd even heard out of him. And those words had filled her with neither pleasure nor hope.

Gerri looked away from him, closed her eyes, let the sun's rays warm her face, listened to the sound of the birds and the fountain's rushing waters.

Des had just admitted he cared about her, but that he wasn't emotionally reliable, and didn't seem inclined to try to change. Where did that leave them?

What she wanted to do was to throw her arms around him, to heal him, to make him all better with her love and affection. It worked with stray cats.

But he wasn't a pet—just a scared, scarred, flawed man. And she couldn't do it, couldn't rescue him. This was his journey, not hers.

It felt as though in the last few days, she'd grown up. Reality wasn't simple, wasn't anywhere near the black and white answers she'd wished for. The "wish" had played a huge part in her metamorphosis; she now knew that there was nothing intrinsically wrong with her.

For years, all Gerri had desired was to look and act and be normal, to be someone other than herself. But she'd found out that who and what she was, while not the norm, was perfectly okay. It was amazing how many lessons she'd learned in these last few days.

She'd let go of an old scar: Tommy's treachery, which had kept her from jumping into the relationship pool for nearly ten years.

She understood now that Rance meant less than zero to her. He'd been nothing more than a teenage crush on the most popular guy in the class. She'd outgrown the crush and had shifted her feelings to a much more complicated man. What she felt for him was real, and deep, and yet, possibly hopeless.

Des returned her feelings. But could he let himself love her? Could he allow himself to trust her feelings for him?

Could he trust that she wouldn't leave him?

She looked at him and smiled, even though her heart was heavy with sadness. "Thanks for your honesty, Des. It means a lot. I understand what you're saying, and I don't have any answers, except that I think people *think* they can't change. I believe people *can* change, but only if they're in enough pain and only if they want it badly enough."

She'd changed, a lot, she knew that for sure. But Des had his own path to follow, and where it would lead, and whether or not it included her, she had no idea.

She stood. "I have to get back to the shop now. So I guess…I'll say goodbye."

The child in her hoped he'd stop her, take her in his arms, declare his undying love and beg her not to leave yet, even to stay with him. Forever.

But both of them lived in the real world, not a fantasy one.

All Des did was nod and say, "Goodbye," a look of such utter despair on his face that she knew she would remember it forever.

Chapter Ten

ONE WEEK LATER: He sat atop the boulder at the mountain's edge, his elbow resting on one bent knee. Major was nearby, being annoyed by a persistent fly. His tail swished back and forth in an attempt to dislodge it.

From up here, he was able to peer down on his acreage, just now visible in the morning light. He'd worked so hard, for so many years, to achieve this. He was proud of what he'd accomplished, proud of the fact that the land was his; the business was slowly prospering. It wasn't a huge spread, but he'd never wanted that. Only his own land, with some cattle and a small house—enough for a decent life. He wasn't a man who craved wealth or anything that came with it.

Down below, he could just make out the house, the outbuildings, the miniature figures of cattle grazing in the pasture. It was springtime, and the past week had been busy. There were several new calves, all healthy—they hadn't lost one.

Again he surveyed his land, but his pleasure in the sight was diminished. He had his home, his spread. He was thirty-five years old.

And he was alone.

When Stella left, he'd given up thinking he wanted someone to share all this with him. And, in truth, he'd thought he was doing just fine.

But that was a lie, one of many he'd been telling himself for most of his life.

He *did* want someone by his side. Someone to talk over the day with, someone to eat meals with and make plans with, to laugh with. Someone to help celebrate the successes and to share in the natural blows that life dealt. Someone to sleep next to in the night and to wake up with in the morning.

He wanted someone... No, not just someone.

Gerri.

He ached with needing her.

Sighing, he rubbed his eyes, which were heavy with lack of sleep. He'd been up most of the night with a pregnant mare who was having a difficult birth. He and a couple of his men had stayed with the suffering animal for hours. It was a breech, and as it was her first foal, the birth canal was tight. Finally, an hour ago, they'd been able to turn the foal just enough to get its rear legs to emerge. The rest of the small animal had followed easily.

Watching that new life spurt forth from all that blood and pain had done something to him. So much determination, so much fight, on both the mother and her foal's part, to live, to exist, to breathe in the air and begin the day.

And as he watched that small newborn animal struggle to get up and take its first steps, he understood and was ashamed at his own cowardice. Despite all the pain surrounding the birth, the foal instinctively knew it deserved a chance at life.

Just as he deserved a chance at life.

He'd been dead inside for years, staying wrapped up in a self-imposed womb of isolation and bitterness. He'd been blind, not only about himself, but about his feelings for Gerri. He'd held himself back, at first because he thought he was protecting her. Bull! He'd been protecting himself.

Then, when he'd realized how much she meant to him, all that rage and jealousy had come up. It was his fault—not Rance's and not Gerri's. The overpowering feelings of possessiveness had been a kind of sickness, caused by his fear of losing her. As he'd lost his mother, and later on, Stella.

Gerri didn't belong in their company. She wasn't his unstable mother or his daydreaming, unhappy wife. She was a separate, totally different human being from either of them. Sweet, trusting, innocent Gerri was all that was good in the world, and he had probably lost her because he'd been too locked up in his past, a prisoner behind walls too thick to see through to the other side.

A butterfly drifted gracefully past his ear and he watched it for a while. He was tired, but after he and his men had made sure the mare and her foal were going to be all right, instead of going to sleep, he'd taken a small notepad and ridden Major up the mountain.

At this moment, Gerri was probably down below on her morning ride. He hadn't spoken with her all week, keeping himself away from the trail in the early morning. Once, he'd seen her as she was returning to the stables, her posture slumped, her face lacking its usual glow. But she hadn't seen him, and he'd kept it that way.

This morning, he had to change all that, unless it really was too late. And if it was, he didn't know what he'd do. What he did know, however, was that he couldn't go back. He was no longer dead inside, not since witnessing the miracle of new life this morning. And if being alive brought with it pain and heartache, then so be it.

Still unsure about his ability to communicate all he'd learned, but knowing he had to make the attempt, he took out his pad and began to write.

She should probably board Ruffy at a different stable, Gerri told herself. It hurt too much riding on Des's land; everywhere she looked, she was reminded of him. All those lovely rides they'd taken together, joking, discussing the issues of the day, getting to know each other. The memories wounded her. Their tree near the creek, the narrow trail between rows of wildflowers. That magical morning on Geiger Peak, when he'd talked about himself for the first time.

Really, it was too hard. She was a masochist to keep doing this to herself. All week, she'd been hoping against hope that she would see him here at his ranch, and that, somehow, things between them would be different.

She needed to accept that it wasn't going to happen, that nothing had changed.

Next week, she told herself, she would snap out of this lethargy and do something about finding a new home for Ruffy, one without all these memories. Frowning, she gazed around her, not even sure where her horse had taken her.

They were at the base of the mountain, the one she'd been remembering moments ago. It was up there, on a boulder looking out onto the entire valley below, where Des had kissed her and made her feel like a woman.

The wrenching in her heart was nearly unbearable. She turned away from the mountain path, heading back to the stables. She had to do something about this awful ache, had to get over him. Next week, she told herself, feeling a tad Scarlett O'Hara-ish. She would deal with the ache next week.

Her reflections were interrupted by the sound of horse's hooves pounding loudly behind her. When she turned in her saddle, she saw Major in the distance, galloping down the final part of the mountain trail.

Des!

Oh, God. Des was coming toward her.

Excitement fought with embarrassment. She wanted to stay and throw her arms around him. Wanted to run away because he might not want her to throw her arms around him. As though her horse had decided to take matters into her own hands, or hooves, Ruffy took off like she'd been spooked by snake. Gerri barely had time to gather the reins in her hands as faster and faster she galloped. Soon, the horse was running at a breakneck speed.

Inexperienced as she was, Gerri grabbed for the saddle horn but, instead, lost control. Scenery whizzed by in a dizzying blur as she tried to keep her balance, tried to pull on the reins, tried to stay upright. One foot slipped out of its stirrup; she felt herself listing to one side and desperately lunged once more for the saddle horn.

Seemingly out of nowhere, Des was there, catching hold of her reins and yanking on them. As quickly as she had bolted, Ruffy came to a sudden stop. Gerri flew out of the saddle.

"Gerri!" she heard Des call as she landed, with a resounding thump, smack on her back. For a moment, she lay there, mortified that she'd fallen off her horse and only secondarily wondering if she'd be paralyzed for life. In the next instant, Des was on his knees beside her, bending over her, his face a mixture of panic and concern.

"Are you all right?"

She turned her head away from him. "Don't know," she mumbled through a suddenly dry mouth. She couldn't bear to look at him.

"Can you move?"

She stirred, rotated her head. There was some throbbing in the back of it, but not too bad. Hesitantly she tried to shift her legs from one side to the other, and, thankfully, they did just that. She wasn't paralyzed, at least. She tried to sit up but she had trouble catching her breath.

Gently Des supported her shoulders and helped her up to a sitting position. She'd had the wind knocked out of her, her butt hurt and her head ached some, but really, that was all.

Except for how ungraceful she must have looked, fighting with her horse for control, then taking a header. More embarrassment flooded her and she buried her face in her hands. "I'm such a klutz."

"No, you're not," Des said sternly. "You have to stop putting yourself down. I've fallen off many times. Let me help you to your feet."

Still unable to face him, she allowed him to assist her. Soon she was upright. Keeping her face averted, she rubbed the back of her head.

"Is it bad?" He sounded concerned.

"Not very."

Cupping her chin, he forced her to look at him. "How many of me do you see?"

She lowered her gaze. "Just one."

"Good. Sure you're okay? Nothing else hurts?"

Only my pride, my self-esteem, my heart.

To her chagrin, she felt her eyes filling with tears. No, she told herself. You will not do that female thing.

She yanked her chin out of his grasp. "I'm fine."

"No, you're not." Taking her by the shoulders, he pulled her to him, his strong arms locking her into an embrace. When she didn't seem inclined to join in, he took her hands and placed her arms around his waist.

"It's okay, you know," he told her. "You can cry."

"But I don't want to!" she wailed, and proceeded to bawl loudly into his shirt. It smelled like a barn, a lovely, earthy smell.

"There, there," he said soothingly, and she gave herself permission to cry out all the anguish and heartache of the past week, right onto the person who was the cause of all that anguish and heartache.

On and on it went, this outpouring of pain. It felt as though the tears would never stop, they would fill up a river and drown them both.

"Shh, sweetheart, I'm here," Des said, stroking her back and head.

Sweetheart? The word registered somewhere in her thoroughly sodden brain.

"Sweetheart?" she croaked. She pulled her tear-stained face away from his chest and gazed into his eyes. Such lovely eyes. So clear today, not clouded with all that turmoil.

"Yes," he said with a half smile, urging her head back onto his shoulder. "Sweetheart," he said, rocking her. "My sweetheart. Oh, Gerri, I've been such an idiot."

Sniffling, she didn't bother to disagree with him; he felt so good, so solid. And besides, he was right, he had been an idiot. So she stayed just where she was until she didn't need to cry anymore. Then she stayed because it felt so good to be there, wrapped up in Des's muscular embrace.

Des had come back! Back to her, back into her life! She honestly hadn't known if he would. And now, here he was. All the past week's suffering was gone now. In its place was a lovely, floating sensation. It felt as if a door had opened, and she went in.

She and Des held on to each other for what seemed like endless minutes. Then he put a finger under her chin, lifted it and kissed her mouth.

It was a warm kiss, a welcoming kiss.

She let herself luxuriate in the feel of his lips, his tongue, and returned his kiss with all the overflowing love in her heart.

"In case you haven't gotten it by now, I love you," he murmured, then kissed her again.

He loved her!

Again, she broke off the kiss and stared at him. "You love me?"

He nodded, his face very serious. "Very much."

"Oh good, because I love you, too."

He blew out a huge, relieved breath, closed his eyes and smiled. "Thank God."

She watched his face, his dear, beloved face, until he opened his eyes and spoke to her again. "I was sure I'd lost you. Can you ever forgive me?"

Just the words she'd been aching to hear all week. "I don't know," she said with a raised eyebrow. "But I'll work on it." Then one side of her mouth quirked up. "Hey, you know me. A pushover. Of course I forgive you, you big idiot!"

He let out a huge peal of laughter and she joined him. It felt so good to laugh, so good to hold on to Des as both their bodies shook with relief and happiness.

"Come," he said, still chuckling as he pulled her over to the bank of the river. It was then that she realized that Ruffy's wild ride had landed them at the cottonwood grove, right next to their tree. How amazing was that?

"Can you sit down?" he asked her, concern back in his gaze.

"Hmm. I'm not sure."

"Well then—"

He scooped her up as though she weighed nothing, and lowered himself onto the ground beneath the tree. He settled her between his bent knees, her backside on his lap. A fleeting memory of being in the same position at last week's poetry evening flickered through Gerri's mind. How tense she'd been then, so unsure of herself. Which made sense, as she'd been on the verge of falling in love with Des and out of love with Rance.

Weird how the two men had traded places, in her mind at least. The fantasy lover had become a friend. The friend had become the real love of her life.

She'd followed her heart.

Thoroughly contented now to be just where she was, Gerri leaned back against Des's chest and rested her head on his shoulder. Most of the pain was gone now, and she closed her eyes, only to open them again when she felt jiggled. It was Des, reaching into his back pocket and pulling out a narrow pad.

"What's that?" she asked him.

He cleared his throat, and she could tell he was just a bit nervous. "Well, I've been doing a lot of thinking, and I, uh, wrote you a poem."

She sat up, which made him groan a bit, and angled her body so she could face him. "You did?"

"Yes, just a little while ago."

"How lovely." Sighing loudly, she turned back around and resumed her former position. "Will you read it to me?"

"It's still kind of rough. I haven't had time to polish it yet."

"I don't care. No one's ever written a poem for me before."

"Wrong." She felt a light kiss on her cheek. "Remember the one I read last Tuesday night? That was about you, too."

"Really?" Again, she sat up and twisted around; again, Des grunted as she did. "Oops. Sorry."

She tried to remember the words of the first poem she'd ever heard Des recite. Something about days and nights and thinking about a woman and feeling despair.

Despair. She'd inspired that? Gerri the klutz? No, no, she would have to stop thinking of herself in those terms. It was no longer okay to make fun of herself.

"Wow," she said again, then leaned back against Des's chest and closed her eyes, her heart soaring with a euphoria she wasn't sure could be contained in that small chamber. "Read to me."

"As long as you stop sitting up so quickly. It kind of, uh, distracts me."

Her eyes flew open again, but she maintained her position; the problem with sitting on Des's lap was that she couldn't see his face. On the other hand, maybe, in this instant, that was okay. "You mean it turns you on?" she asked.

He chuckled. "You noticed."

Heat rose to her face as she said, "Couldn't really miss it, could I? Kind of like that old joke, 'Is that a banana in your pocket, or are you just glad to see me?'"

His chest moved up and down as he chuckled some more. She swallowed, then went for it. "Maybe, uh, later, we can, you know—'' She broke off, unable to finish the request.

"Make love?" Des whispered in her ear. "Is that what you mean?" When she nodded mutely, he said, "I had a similar thought myself."

"Ah, good. And Des?" She held her breath and bit her lip, really glad now that they couldn't see each other's faces, and confessed, "I may be a little out of practice, so don't expect too much of me."

"Oh, Gerri," he said, a smile in his voice as he ran his hand up and down her arm. It tingled from his touch. "I'm pretty sure we'll both be just fine."

"Well, if you're sure—?"

"I'm sure."

From behind, he wound his arms around her waist and pulled her tightly to him, nuzzling her neck. Then one of his hands gently cupped her breast, and she felt the tip of it spring to attention, felt the rest of her body's quickening response. There was no mistaking Des's arousal, for sure, and her own was keeping pace pretty well. Being desired by Des, and knowing that the strength of her own desire matched his, felt utterly, totally wonderful. Who needed magic?

Suddenly she remembered what was in his other hand. The pad. "Wait a minute. You were about to read me my poem."

He was still exploring her neck. "Why don't we fool around a little first?" he murmured, making her shiver.

Primly, she removed his hand from her breast and placed it back on her waistline. Then she leaned back and closed her eyes, her hand on top of his free one. "Poem first, please."

"If you insist," he said with an exaggerated sigh. "Delayed gratification can be a pretty nice turn-on."

She slapped his hand playfully. "Read."

"Okay, then, here goes."

There is rust around the hinges of my soul
They creak when I try to open it up,
So I let it fall closed again,
Afraid of the sound,
Afraid that when I do open it
There will be nothing there.
"It needs oil," she says.
"Let me be the oil."
But I am afraid
And so, it remains closed.
Except...there is a noise.
There is something beneath the cover.
It wants to come out of hiding,
Like a foal writhing to be born.
"No," I say.
"I won't let what's beneath the cover
Come into the day."
"But you must," she says.
"You cannot stop birth;
To be born is the only chance we have
To be alive."
So, together we lubricate the hinges.
Together we pull at the cover, trying to open
it up.
But it won't move.
"See?" I say, "it's stuck."
"It's impossible," I say.
"I am afraid," I say again.

"More oil," she says.

"Let the oil seep around the rust, fill in the cracks.

Let it clean the decay."

But I am afraid and give up.

Again, cursed woman, she won't let me.

"Here," she tells me. "See?

I have applied more oil and it is ready."

No one, in all the world, can know the dread that surrounds me.

I want to run, but I know I cannot,

As slowly, gently, she pulls at the cover.

And yes the hinges creak

And yes, they protest

But then

They give

And the cry of life pierces the morning sky.

Total silence greeted the ending of his poem. Des waited, nervous as hell and not daring to breathe.

When he heard Gerri say, with a catch in her throat, "Oh, Des, it's beautiful," when she shifted her position so that she faced him, straddling his legs, and threw her arms around his neck and hugged him, he knew that she'd understood what he was trying to tell her. Not that the message in his poem was difficult to understand, especially for someone with Gerri's brilliant mind and soft, loving heart. But still...she had heard him.

He rested his forehead on her shoulder, unbearably moved by the moment and the woman who held on to him as though he were a precious gift that she couldn't let go of. His voice hoarse with emotion, he told her, "Like I said last week, Gerri, I'm pretty scarred. And terrified, too. But no one, in all my life, has affected me the way you do. I'm willing to try to make a go of it, if you'll put up with me."

Raising her head, she met his gaze. He could see the wheels turning in her busy brain as she contemplated his words. "Hmm. Well. What I think is that we're both pretty scarred," she said quietly. "But what is it they say about love healing all wounds? You've already healed a lot of mine. Let me do the same for you."

Then she smiled, the light of love and the sweetness of her soul shining from her eyes. Like an ancient soothing balm, her light, gentle spirit healed him, brought him back to life after so many years in hell.

"We'll make it, Des," she said softly. "I know we will. Trust me."

As he brought her face closer to his for another kiss, he murmured, "That's just it, my love. I do."

Epilogue

The wedding was a small affair, held at the ranch. Gerri's folks flew in, as did her brother and his wife, and an aunt and uncle. The ranch hands were there, as were a few of Gerri's friends, including the maid of honor, Didi. Des's brothers and their families came.

Even Rance was there. In the six months since Gerri and Des had sat beneath the tree and he'd allowed her into his heart, he and Rance had actually struck up a friendship of sorts.

Rance wasn't a bad guy, something Gerri knew and Des was finding out, just someone who had had it too easy all his life. She wondered what would happen if and when things no longer fell into his lap with minimal effort on his part. Would he be able to cope?

The ceremony had been beautiful. And she'd looked pretty good herself, Gerri had to admit, in a simple white gown, and with a new short haircut that

actually behaved itself, and really did frame her face
well. At Des's request, she'd worn only a little
makeup, and the only jewelry was the ring he placed
on her finger, an antique circle of yellow gold and
diamonds she and Des had picked out at Didi's shop.

Des, all spruced up in his wedding finery, had been
a knockout. Gerri had had to catch her breath when
she saw him in his dark blue suit, silver tie and new
boots. Imagine, she thought as the ceremony began,
Phoebe Minerva "Gerri" Conklin, soon to be Quinlan, with a catch like Desmond O'Bannion Quinlan.

The nicest part of all, of course, was that he thought
she was a major catch, too. Neither could believe their
luck in finding each other, which boded well for their
future together.

After the ceremony, there had been champagne and
toasts, with Gerri's father quoting liberally from
everyone from Shakespeare to John Lennon on the
subject of Love and Wedding Customs, until her
mother had gently suggested he yield the floor to hear
what others had to say. This he had done with grace,
but not before his eyes filled and he toasted his daughter and her excellent new husband.

Gerri's eyes filled too at the sight of her dear egg-
head father being patted on the back by her beloved
mother. Theirs was a marriage to emulate, and she
was pretty sure she and Des could do it.

After that, there had been more champagne, more
toasts and lots of wonderful food. Now the party was
in full swing. Out on the patio, Gerri and Rance
danced to lively music supplied by a piano, guitar and
fiddle.

Rance shook his head mournfully. "You know,

Gerri, you could have had me instead of that cowboy." But he said it with a lightheartedness that let her know he was kidding.

"Nonsense. I'd have driven you crazy within a week."

"Maybe I'd have driven you crazy a lot sooner. Well, anyway, I'm happy for you, really, Mrs. Quinlan. You two look good together. The ceremony made me want to get hitched myself."

"That would sure please your mother."

He winced. "Don't remind me."

"Anyone special in mind?"

"Afraid not."

She studied him for a while as he led her around the floor. Yes, she thought. He's the next one.

"Listen here, Rance," she told him, "when Des and I get back from our honeymoon, stop by the store. I have a little present for you."

One blond eyebrow arched. "Oh? And what would that be?"

"A pair of eyeglasses."

"A what?"

Des tapped Rance on the shoulder. "Cutting in. I want to dance with my wife."

As Gerri shifted over to her husband's arms, her heart filled with exquisite pleasure. "My husband," she said proudly, then kissed him. Arms locked around each other, they continued to kiss as Des whirled them away.

She heard Rance calling after her, "But, Gerri, I don't need glasses."

She interrupted kissing her husband long enough to call back to him, with a mysterious smile, "You may not think you do, Rance. But I have a feeling that one day, you will.''

* * * * *

Silhouette Romance presents tales of
enchanted love and things beyond explanation
in the heartwarming series,

Soulmates

Couples destined for each other are brought
together by the powerful magic of love....

The second time around
brings an unexpected suitor, in

THE WISH

by Diane Pershing (on sale April 2003)

The power of love battles a medieval spell, in

THE KNIGHT'S KISS

by Nicole Burnham (on sale May 2003)

Soulmates

Some things are meant to be....

*Available at
your favorite retail outlet.*

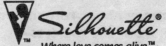

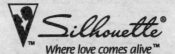

In April 2003
Silhouette Books and bestselling author

MAGGIE SHAYNE

invite you to return to the world of
Wings in the Night
with

TWO BY TWILIGHT

Enjoy this brand-new story!
Run from Twilight

Savor this classic tale!
Twilight Vows

Find these seductive stories, as well as all the other tales of dark
desire in this haunting series, at your favorite retail outlet.

Silhouette®
Where love comes alive™

COMING NEXT MONTH

#1660 WITH HIS KISS—Laurey Bright

He was back in town! Gunther "Steve" Stevens had always unsettled
Triss Allerdyce—and he'd been secretly jealous of her marriage to his
much older mentor. But now her husband's will brought them together
again, and Steve's anger soon turned to love. But would that be enough
to awaken the hidden passions of this Sleeping Beauty?

#1661 THE WEDDING ADVENTURE—Melissa McClone

The *last* thing Cade Armstrong Waters wanted to do was spend two
weeks on a tropical island with socialite Cynthia Sterling! But with
his charity organization at stake, he agreed to the crazy scheme. Sur-
viving Cynthia's passionate kisses with his heart intact was another
story....

#1662 THE NANNY SOLUTION—Susan Meier
Daycare Dads

Nanny Hannah Evans was going to give millionaire Jake Malloy
a piece of her mind! It was bad enough the sexy single father was running around like a government spy, but now she was actually falling
for her confounding boss. Was he *ever* going to give up his secret dou-
ble life for fatherhood and...love?

#1663 THE KNIGHT'S KISS—Nicole Burnham
Soulmates

Thanks to a medieval curse, Nick Black had been around for a
long time...a *long* time. Researching ancient artifacts for Princess
Isabella diTalora, he hoped to find the answers to break the spell.
But would he find the one woman who could break the walls around
his heart?

#1664 CAPTIVATING A COWBOY—Jill Limber

So city girl Julie Kerns broke her collarbone trying to fix up her
grandmother's cottage—she could *hire* someone to help, right? But
what if he was ex-Navy SEAL Tony Graham—a man sexy as sin who
kissed like heaven? Maybe that cottage would need *a lot* more work
than she first thought....

#1665 THE BACHELOR CHRONICLES—Lissa Manley

Jared Warfield was torn between his pride in his business and the need
for privacy to adopt his orphaned baby niece. So he planned to show
fiesty reporter Erin James all about the store—and nothing about himself. But the best-laid plans went awry when the unlikely couple finally met!

SRCNM0403